More than a Promise

More than a Promise

than a

Promise

ROMANCE IN RIDGEVIEW ♥ BOOK 2

Amy Green

More than a Promise
Book 2 in the Romance in Ridgeview Series

ROMANCE IN RIDGEVIEW

Breaking the Best Friend Code

More than a Promise

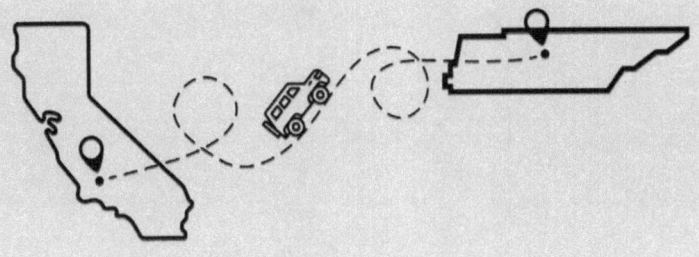

To anyone who's ever felt like they're too much,
don't ever dim your sparkle.
We need you.

WHAT PEOPLE ARE SAYING

A *laugh out loud* take

on *enemies to lovers*

filled with tension, yearning, and

a crew of fast talking friends

finding their way in the world.

Olivia Hope McCarthy,
author of *New River Gorge(ous)*

CONTENT WARNINGS

Reading is a very personal experience and what may trigger some won't trigger others. Before you read this book please be aware of some subjects that are contained.

- On and off page panic attacks and talks of anxiety
- On and off page talks of cancer (parent: past, patients: MMC is an oncology nurse)
- Parental abandonment (past)
- Anaphylaxis—I promise its in a respectful and humorous way
- Third Act Breakup—I know! I hate it too, but the story needed it
- Character's disdain for Hootie and and the Blowfish—nothing personal, love you Darius!

Torrance

9 Years Ago

NOTHING COMPARES TO the scent of industrial disinfectant, sweat, and stale pizza. The lights on the roller rink take on a life of their own as the 80's music blares. My best friends really went all out this year to surprise me. As much as a birthday straight out of Xanadu is a dream come true, the real surprise was Jonathan flying in from New York. It wouldn't have felt like my birthday without him. I know there will come a day that we don't celebrate our birthdays together, but today is not that day.

I tighten my skates and slide over towards Millie and Jonathan, the sequins on my shorts catching the lights and making a disco ball effect. Right as I make the split-second decision to burst between my friends, I run into a hard body, knocking me to the ground.

"Do you mind?" A deep, not-so-happy voice says. I look up to see a frowning face looking down at me. I don't know what it is about this stranger, but I snap.

"Maybe if you were watching where you were going," I say with all the snark I can muster. Who does this guy think he is? He ran into me. I'm the one on the ground. He could at least help me up, but nope. That's too much for this Prince Charming.

Millie and Jonathan turn at the commotion. Jonathan extends a hand and helps me up. I hear a rip. The wheel of my skates caught on my sparkle tights and now there's a huge hole. Just great.

"Are you okay?" Millie rushes to my side.

"Yeah, I'm fine. No harm done, unless you count my tights." I dust off my behind. I don't think there is anything there, but with sequins and questionably-cleaned carpets you can never be too careful. I see the guy who knocked me down walking towards the concession stand. "Some jerk knocked me down."

An hour later, I'm dripping sweat and smiling ear-to-ear as I skate with my friends, my crash with the jerk a distant memory.

"I need water!" I yell over the music. Everyone nods and heads towards the rink exit and our reserved table.

"Sorry, we're late!" my roommate Kiersten says as she sinks into the seat next to me. "Practice ran long. I just couldn't get that triple axel tonight!"

I wrap her in a hug. "You could have stayed home. You must be exhausted."

"No way! I wouldn't miss your birthday!"

"Okay, but no pressure to skate. Your legs have to be killing you after being on the ice all afternoon."

"It's not too bad actually," she laughs. "Where's Amara?"

I look around for our other roommate, "I don't know. I haven't seen her in awhile. She said she was going to meet up with some guy from one of her classes."

Kiersten rolls her eyes. "She brought a date to *your* birthday party?"

I shrug. "It's not that big of a deal, besides it's the first time seeing him outside of class. What better way to get a read on the guy if not in a very public place?"

Jonathan plops down beside me and steals my water bottle.

"Hey! I was drinking that!"

He takes a long swig. "Not anymore."

I shove him in the arm.

Millie walks over and hands me a new bottle. "Joke's on him. I was bringing over a bottle straight from the cooler, but now it's yours."

I take the bottle and do a little victory dance.

Jonathan is about to respond when he spots Amara and who I can only assume is the guy from her class. She sees us, and they make their way over.

"There you are," she says with a bright smile. "I lost track of you guys while you were on the floor."

"You wouldn't have lost track of us if you would have been out there with us," I goad. I know she won't skate; her parents are over protective and would absolutely lose it if anything happened to her.

"I was talking with Duncan." She motions to the guy behind her. "Duncan, this is everybody. Everybody, this is Duncan. We have English 101 together."

There is a collective hello followed by a slew of overlapping conversations. It's all chaotic perfection until I see the jerk who ran into me earlier making his way towards us. What is it with this guy? He didn't finish the job the first time?

"There you are!" Duncan claps Jerk Man on the shoulder. "This is my roommate, Porter."

Duncan introduces him to the group. Everyone says hello, oblivious to the fact that Porter and I are seemingly in a stare down. He might have knocked me down earlier, but this round I'm going to win.

CHAPTER 1

Torrance

*I*T'S OFFICIAL: I hate weddings. Call me jaded. Call me cynical. I've heard it all before, but even as I sit here watching my best friend marry the man of her dreams, the man who she's loved basically all of her life, I still don't get the appeal.

Don't get me wrong, I'm beyond happy for Millie. She's been my best friend since we were twelve. She's also a hopeless romantic. The type that Hallmark movies are made for. You know the type; they are sure life will go their way because in the end love always wins. Even when they endure heartbreak or things don't go according to plan, they know that whatever is meant to be will be in the end. I hope she and Mark are happy. Heaven help him if she's not because I will destroy him. Gladly.

I watch as they smile at each other dopily and know that if ever two people could be considered soul mates, it's these two. I might have had my doubts when they first started dating, but I've seen how much Mark cares for Millie and, more importantly, how much he cherishes her. It's almost enough to change my mind about love.

I work hard, and I play hard. I don't leave room for romantic entanglements. Over the years I have cultivated a system that works for me. I started it back in high school when I saw all my friends lose their minds trying to figure out if their crush liked them back. I wasn't about that life. I had goals and things I wanted to achieve before I even looked for that "someone special." I date but nothing serious and pretty much never more than three weeks. The few times that I've gone more than three weeks with any one guy, it's always ended in heartbreak. It's only happened twice, but I will not allow myself to go through that again.

Now, at the ripe age of twenty-seven, I do what I've trained myself to do. I run. Literally and metaphorically. I figure as long as I keep moving, I'll never notice what I'm missing, or at the very least I won't dwell on it. I figure if everyone is right, and love always finds a way, then it's going to have to woo me. I'm going to have to be fully and completely swept off my feet, and there has to be one hundred percent certainty that it's the real deal. I refuse to waste my time.

I LOATHE MOVING. Even if it is only down the hall in the same house. I still have to move all of my stuff and put it away again. It's annoying and tedious. At least I don't have to move any furniture. I guess there's one positive to your best friend and now-former roommate moving in with her new husband. She doesn't need the furniture that was in her room.

The biggest adjustment? Having my own room. I haven't had my own room since my little sister Carson was born when I was four. When I went to college, I had roommates. Luckily for me, I hit the roommate jackpot, and Kiersten and I instantly bonded. When all my roommates would go home for the summer, I would stay with my roommate Amara's grandparents in their makeshift second bedroom. In hindsight I don't think it was really a bedroom but more like a sitting room. It was right off the kitchen and was the only way to the backyard, but it had a pullout bed and a closet. And the rent was cheap.

"Is this the last of it?" Jonathan, one of my best friends since middle school, asks. "Please tell me this is all of it. I'm so done moving things."

I give him a sardonic smile. "You make it sound like we've made you do manual labor."

"Look, you moving rooms was easy, but I've already helped move all of Millie's things into Mark's place. And before that, I was helping move all sorts of furniture in Mark's place making room for Millie to move in. You'd think if you were getting married you would have planned ahead."

I try to hold in my laugh. As much as Jonathan was against Millie and his brother, Mark, getting together, even he has to admit they are a match made in heaven.

"It's not like they had a long engagement. Besides, he just moved back to Ridgeview six months ago. Pretty sure Millie kept complaining that he hadn't even unpacked everything. How much work did you really have to do?"

"I know, but still."

"Weren't Millie's brothers there to help?"

"You know, it's annoying when you spout off all the facts like a know-it-all."

I grin over at him. "I know."

He rolls his eyes.

"When does Trina move into your old room?"

"I think tomorrow, but it might not be until Tuesday. It all depends on when she can borrow her brother's truck."

I've met Trina a few times through Millie since they work together, and from what I can tell, she will fit right in with our whole roommate situation. But she still isn't Millie. I really am happy for Millie, but her getting married and moving out is hitting me harder than I was prepared for.

"How do you feel about it? It's been the four of you for nine years. That's a long time."

"It is a long time, but I think it will be good. We've all met her and got to know her a little bit at the wedding."

Jonathan nods. "Hey, you'll finally have someone to go to clubs with. She seems like someone who would be into that."

"Maybe," I shrug. Though it's not like I go to regular clubs. The places I go to are more likely considered bars. Though they still don't draw your usual bar crowd. It's hard to explain. None of my roommates ever went with me when I invited them so I stopped asking if they wanted to come. Jonathan has gone a few times, but it all depends on his schedule. He teaches at our alma mater, taking over the choir and theater programs when our teacher retired a couple years ago.

"I'm not saying you have to invite her, but, Tor, it's not a terrible idea to let someone you live with see that side of your life."

I know he's right, but I'm just stubborn enough to not give him the satisfaction of agreeing with him.

"I think we should focus more on the fact that you can't date her," I tease.

"I don't see that happening, because the only person who dates less than me is you. No more dating bans. I've learned my lesson."

"Good. I can't handle being in the middle of all that drama again."

Jonathan, Millie, and I might go way back, but the two of them go back even further, like to before they were born. Somehow along the way a deal was made that they wouldn't date each other's siblings, which all came crashing down when his brother moved back to town and fell hard for Millie. They dated in secret, and it got messy. Jonathan and Millie almost lost their lifelong friendship over it. In the end it all worked out, but it sucked being in the middle of it when it was dicey.

"I promise to keep all of my drama to myself."

"That's all I ask...unless it's high school drama with your students. Then you know I want all the details. It's like my own personal reality show."

I duck right before I get hit in the head with a pillow.

CHAPTER 2

Torrance

*I*F I HAVE to look at one more picture of Hawaii, I'm going to lose it. I'm so excited that Millie is back from her honeymoon, and I'm glad she and Mark had a good time, but for the love, stop it with the pictures! We get it! You're in love. You had fun. You'd love to go back, but do I really need to relive every last minute with you?

This is Millie, so we aren't getting *all* the details, thank goodness. Ain't nobody want to hear about your wedded bliss. Jonathan is barely keeping it together with all the kissing pictures. Okay, that is kind of amusing. Nevermind, keep them coming.

"I missed all of you!" Millie gushes. "It's so weird being back in this house knowing that at the end of the night I'll go somewhere else."

She starts to tear up because of course she does. Millie is nothing if not sentimental. On anyone else I'd find it annoying, but on her, it's just endearing and so…Millie.

"I know!" Amara exclaims. "It's always been just the four of us living together."

"How are things going with Trina?" Millie asks.

"Really good," Kiersten answers. And they have been. She really fits right in. She's just enough like Millie that it feels like we've all known each other for years but different enough that it doesn't feel like she's trying to replace her. It's honestly the best situation.

"I'm sad she wasn't able to be here tonight," Millie frowns. Oh, my dear, sweet, emotional child.

"She has a date, but I know she's going to want all the details of your trip when you see her at work," Kiersten says.

Millie nods, then looks at the clock. "I really should be going."

She stands, and we all huddle in for a group hug. This feels so weird!

"I'll walk out with you," Jonathan says as he links arms with Millie like we all have a thousand times.

After they leave, Amara and Kiersten head towards their rooms, and I stay sitting in silence. Why is all this change hitting me so hard? It's not like I didn't know that we would all start going our separate ways eventually. And it's not like Millie is that far away. She's still in Ridgeview. It's not like she died. She's very much alive. She's just married. Living across town. With a man. A man that is her husband. It's all perfectly normal.

"Hey, you." Kiersten plops next to me on the couch. "You okay?"

"Yeah, why wouldn't I be?"

"Because things are changing. Millie moved out. She's married. And if Duncan actually proposes this time, then Amara isn't too far behind."

I shrug. I know it sounds terrible, but part of me doesn't think Duncan will go through with it. I mean, they've been dating for years. And I do mean *years*. Like since our freshman year of college. They claim to be madly in love, but their relationship hasn't changed much in all that time. At least that's what it looks like on the outside. I'd love nothing more than to be proven wrong, but skeptic, remember?

Duncan is a nice enough guy. I'd consider him a friend. He's just...how do I put it nicely? Kind of blah. I've just always thought Amara would be with someone as hyper-focused and motivated as she is. It's not everyone who can double major, graduate early, and then on top of it all to not only get into the top medical schools in the country but have them basically start a bidding war over her. I could be dramatizing it a bit, but the point is, Amara is crazy smart, and everyone knows it.

"Just between us," I double check that Amara isn't coming down the hall. "Do you think Duncan is actually going to propose this time? He's been saying he's going to for almost two years now."

"You just don't want to be forced to spend time with Porter," Kiersten accuses. I mean, she's not wrong. Duncan's best friend and long-time roommate, Porter Collins, is basically the bane of my existence.

"I can't help it! He bugs the everlasting crap out of me!"

Kiersten laughs. "I don't know why. He's a nice guy."

"You think everyone is nice," I say dryly.

"Not everyone."

"Yes, little Miss Sunshine, you do. Even people who don't deserve it, like that loser of an ex of yours."

"Now there's no need to bring Topher into this. That was years ago."

"You're only proving my point. Topher the Gopher messed you up royally, and you still won't let anyone talk bad about him. If anyone deserves to have something bad said about them, then it is the guy who was stupid enough to not only cheat on you but then rub his new relationship in your face."

"How did we even get into this argument?!" Kiersten shouts. "Look, I get it, I choose to see the good in people even when not everyone is always good, but it's better than being cynical about everything!"

I shut my mouth before I can retort. Did Kiersten just get mad at me? I've finally done it. I've pushed her too hard. I'm about to apologize for overstepping when Kiersten speaks again.

"I'm sorry. That wasn't fair of me to lose my temper like that. I know you love me and only want the best for me." She takes my hand and gives it a squeeze. "All those feelings about everything with Topher are still so raw, you know. I know he was a jerk. And what he did was the lowest of lows, but I just can't dwell on that. I need to see the good in life, you know. Or else— well, if I don't then things get pretty dark, and that isn't how I want to live my life. Life is too short and too fragile to spend it being angry about things you can't change."

I bite the inside of my cheek in order to hold back the emotions that are fighting tooth and nail to escape. She's right, life is too short, but I will not let that dam break. Not today. And not with Kiersten, even if she is the one person I know who would fully understand.

"I'm the one who should apologize. I shouldn't have pushed you so hard. Just because I can't find anything positive to say about pesky Porter Collins doesn't mean you should be as cynical as I am. I guess I'm just envious how easy it is for you to naturally assume that there is good in everything."

We sit in a huddled cuddle like we usually do when we have a heart to heart, then Kiersten heads to her room for the night. I say I'm going to do the same, but I know I won't go to sleep anytime soon. Sleep never comes easy. It's at night when I'm alone that my thoughts begin to race. Tonight is no different. When sleep does come, it's full of the nightmares that plague me. After waking up in a cold sweat, I finally just get up and go for a run.

CHAPTER 3

Porter

"ARE YOU ACTUALLY going to propose this time?" I ask Duncan as he lounges on my couch staring at the ceiling.

He shifts to look at me. "Do you think I shouldn't?"

"It shouldn't matter what I think. It's a matter of if you love Amara and want to marry her. Because proposing means you will be getting married."

"I know that!"

"Do you? Because from where I'm standing, you've been in the same war with yourself for the last two years."

"Are you saying I shouldn't propose and just keep the status quo?"

"I didn't say that."

"But you didn't not say that."

I stand up and head towards my kitchen. I might as well meal prep while Duncan has his existential crisis in my living room.

"Don't go putting words in my mouth so that you can hear what you want me to say." Sometimes being friends with Duncan is way too exhausting. "I'm just saying don't lead her on. Nine years is a long time, and I saw how Amara got all doe-eyed at Millie's wedding."

"Amara did seem pretty into that wedding, huh? They all were."

"Not all of them," I mutter.

Duncan snickers. "You wouldn't be talking about a certain green-eyed vixen, now, would you?"

"Vixen? Really?" I roll my eyes as I pull out a cutting board and a knife. "Not exactly how I would describe Torrance Rodriguez."

"And how would you describe Tori?"

Annoying. Aggravating. Loud. Know-it-all. She has this way of just glaring into your soul that just makes your stomach churn. "I haven't thought too much about it."

"Mmm-hmm. Sure." Even from the other side of my studio apartment, I don't like the look he's giving me. "If you say so."

I know better than to argue with him on this, but I can't leave it alone. It's like a scab I have to pick. "She's nothing but rude and judgmental, and I don't care to waste my time dwelling on the subject any longer."

Duncan doesn't even try to hide his snicker.

From the moment I met Torrance, she has been on my last nerve. Sure, she's objectively beautiful on the outside, but it's what's on the inside that puts me in knots.

Unfortunately, the universe just keeps on finding ways to throw us together. From the classes we had together in college to the fact that her roommate has been dating my best friend for almost a decade. No matter where I go or what I do there is always a chance that Torrance will show up at some point.

I finish meal prepping for the week much more aggressively than is warranted, but the chopping is cathartic. At some point during the process, Duncan grows bored and takes off, which honestly is the greatest gift he could give me. All this talk about weddings and engagements. No, thank you. Look, I'm not against it. I just don't think it's for me.

I check my watch. I have twenty minutes until I pick up my dogs from their grooming appointments, and then it's dinner on the way to the hospital.

TONIGHT'S SHIFT HAS been brutal. I typically love my job. It's not easy by any means, but oncology is where I belong. Tonight, however, we were short three nurses which multiplied my workload exponentially.

I have a routine. I like my routine. I know I'm in a field where you need to adapt quickly, but that doesn't mean I have to like it. To add to everything, my favorite patient has taken a turn for the worse, and every time I go in and check on her, I put every last ounce of energy I have into keeping her spirits up. I know Willa doesn't expect me to, but she reminds me so much of my mom that it's almost an impulse.

"How are you feeling, Willa?" I ask as I walk into the room. I make quick work of checking her levels and making the necessary notes.

Willa pats my arm. "About the same as I was the last time you came in to check on me, fifteen minutes ago." She gives me a knowing smile. "Come, sit. Let's talk."

"Oh, I don't really have time to chat right now."

"Porter, if you have time to come and check on me every fifteen minutes, you have time to sit and chat for five."

I smile as I pull up a chair. "Are Brody and Bella going to be able to visit this weekend?"

Willa's face lights up at the mention of her children. "Oh, yes! And it's a long weekend so they will be here through Tuesday."

She continues to tell me all about her children. About Brody's fiancée and how they are starting to plan the wedding. And how Bella has a new boyfriend, but Willa isn't too sure about him yet. Five minutes comes and goes, and just like that, I need to go make my rounds and check on my other patients.

"I've got to get going. I'll come check on you in a couple hours."

Willa nods. "I'm not going anywhere."

I walk out of the room towards the nurse's station.

"How's Willa doing tonight?" Our shift manager, Carol, asks.

"She's in good spirits." I pause. "Considering."

Carol looks up from her computer. "This job can be hard, Porter. If you need to take some time off to clear your head, I strongly advise you to do so."

I square my shoulders as I look her in the eye. "I know this job is hard, but taking time off isn't going to make it less hard. I won't leave my patients."

It's the same not-quite-an-argument we have often. I know Carol means well, but I also feel like she thinks I'm less of a nurse purely because I'm male. It's as if she thinks I can't come to care for my patients and still do my job. I can. I know better than most people what it's like to spend so much time with a cancer patient. Half of high school was spent doing my homework next to my mom's hospital bed. It was those nurses who made me want to go into medicine in the first place.

"You have to take time off eventually," Carol argues. "You already have more weeks accumulated than is recommended. Anymore and I'm going to have to force you to take time off."

I just nod. I know I never take time off. I should, but I don't. I'm saving up the time so I can take Mom on her dream trip to France. Her recent scans came back clear, which means she's been in remission for a full year. Part of me wants to bite the bullet and take her now, but another part wants to be sure it won't come back again. Not that there are any guarantees when it comes down to it. I know this, but I still sit in decision-making paralysis. It's almost like if I don't make the decision then time won't pass, and she will remain as she is now. Healthy and in remission.

"At least take a weekend off. Go do something fun with friends. Go on a date," Carol continues. She's really not letting this go tonight.

"I'll think about it."

"Well, that's better than your usual reply," Carol says dryly.

I give her a thumbs up as I walk away.

The rest of the night is relatively uneventful. I check in on Willa a couple more times, but she's sleeping, and I don't want to disturb her. The similarities between her and my mom really are almost eery. Both single moms with two children—a boy and a girl— both having gone through remission and then the cancer coming back. It's probably why I'm so worried about her. It's like living through my mom's treatments all over again. I can't even imagine what Brody and Bella are going through being so far away while she's here.

When Mom's cancer first came back, I had just graduated from high school. I had planned to go straight to college, but once the diagnosis came in, I couldn't leave. I had to be there. My little sister was only ten. She needed me just as much as Mom did. So I stayed.

I stayed home and worked for two years. Once she was back in remission, I did everything I could to get through school as quickly as possible. I had originally planned on going to medical school, but I could get through nursing school faster. And since working with patients was my main priority, it made sense. I haven't regretted that decision one bit. I love what I do, even when it's taxing. I decided last year to start working towards becoming a physician assistant, so when I'm not at work, I'm studying.

Duncan says I don't have a life, but what he really means is I don't have a life like he thinks I should. He thinks I should date more than I do. It's not like I'm a monk. I date. Just not the same girl. I'm great at first dates; it's the second or third when I usually lose interest. There just hasn't been a woman who I've thought worth the time to pursue anything further. No one catches my attention. My grandmother, MarMar, says I'm looking in the wrong places, but she never seems to find it prudent to tell me where I should be looking. So it's just some sort of guessing game. And I don't do guessing games.

> **TRENT:** Dude, come out with us tonight!

> **PORTER:** I'm assuming this was meant for someone else.

> **TRENT:** No, this was very much meant for you, Cuz.

> **PORTER:** I hate when you call me that.

> **TRENT:** Then come out with us tonight, Cuz.

> **PORTER:** At least spell it correctly. It's cousin. Not Cuz.

> **TRENT:** Has anyone ever told you you have the personality of a wet blanket?

> **PORTER:** You. Many, many times.

He might be family, but he's super annoying.

> **PORTER:** I have work tonight.

> **TRENT:** No, you don't. It's Thursday. You don't work on Thursdays.

Darn Trent and his memory! Why is this something he remembers? He can't remember that he broke his arm when he was seven, but my work schedule? Sure, easy peasy. I know when I'm beat, and honestly getting out of the house doesn't sound too bad. And I do like hanging out with my cousin, even if it doesn't seem like it. He's one of my best friends. We didn't get to see each other growing up as much as I saw our cousin, Nic, but we're all pretty close thanks to MarMar.

> **PORTER:** When and where?

> **TRENT:** Really?!

> **PORTER:** When and where before I change my mind.

Trent texts me a time and a place. I'm already dreading it. It's a club. I hate clubs. I especially hate going to clubs with Trent and his friends. Women will be hanging around all night, and not the ones that I really care to get to know. Sure, some of them can have a stimulating conversation, but most are just interested in the possibility of hooking up with a professional athlete. Did I mention that Trent is a pro football player? Because yeah. Not only is my cousin annoying when it comes to remembering details, he's also annoyingly good-looking, built like a house, charismatic, and talented. I, on the other hand, am not bad looking, but you aren't going to see my face on any toothpaste ads. I have a much leaner build, and many would say I don't have enough people skills to be considered charismatic. Okay, so only one person has ever told me the last part, and to be fair, Torrance Rodriguez really is the worst, so her opinion doesn't matter.

I hang back from the rest of the group, mostly comprised of Trent's teammates and their entourage, while they go, in the words of Trent, "get into the groove" on the dance floor. The only one not joining in is the team captain, Ryan McConnell. I like Ryan. He's one member of the team I could actually see being friends with without Trent being around. The rest of the guys are nice enough, but football was never really my sport. I only ever watched it growing up when Trent was around. Now I only watch when Trent is playing.

Ryan taps my knee and nods his head towards a group of three women heading our way. "Incoming. You ready for this?"

"No, but it's what I get for coming out with you guys."

Ryan grins. "It's not all bad." He leans in closer to whisper, "Just do what I do. Use really big words. It usually weeds out the ones you don't want to talk to."

I snort. "That's actually rather genius."

Ryan leans back into his spot. "I didn't graduate from MIT for nothing."

"I always forget that you went there. You should really mention going there more often," I tease.

"You know, I really should," Ryan grins.

The next several minutes follow the usual pattern. The group of women come over with the subtlety of a bomb, although much less complex. They recognize Ryan and are instantly all over him. I'll give the guy credit, even when he's not interested in who's talking to him, he's still polite. They might not walk away with his number or an offer to go "hang out," but they still leave thinking this interaction was the highlight of their night.

This pattern repeats several more times throughout the night, although some groups are larger and some smaller. The larger groups usually come by when more of the team is at the table.

"Porter!" I hear my name yelled from across the mezzanine where our table is located. My head jerks up. I'm not expecting anyone I know to be here. But it all makes sense when I see the tall blonde come bounding towards me with her arms open wide and a huge smile on her face.

I barely stand up before she barrels into me.

"I can't believe you actually came! It's so good to see you!"

I hug her back. She might be loud and a little much at times, but Trent's girlfriend is a good one. "Hey, Sloane."

She releases me and starts jumping up and down excitedly.

"Since you're here I can *finally* introduce you to my bestie!" She squeals. It's then that I see the dark-haired woman standing behind her. Sloane grabs her friend's arm and pulls her closer to me. "Porter, this is Zayna. She's a graphic designer and loves all things dogs. You two have so much in common! I'm so excited about this!" She looks between the two of us and squeals again. "Did you know that not only do both of you love dogs, but you both have multiple dogs?"

"How could we? We just met. Sort of," Zayna says dryly.

If Sloane notices her friend's sarcasm, she doesn't give any indication. "And you both run! Like, how crazy is that?"

Zayna rolls her eyes. "Yes, because running is such a strange thing for people to do."

Sloane looks as if she is going to argue, but she gets interrupted as Trent swoops in behind her and wraps her up in a big hug. She squeals again, and the two of them start displaying way too much PDA for comfort. It's actually rather uncomfortable. Zayna must be more used to it than I am since she just sidesteps where they have planted and comes over to me.

"Hi. I'm pretty sure all of that before was Sloane's way of introducing us. I'm Zayna."

I take her outstretched hand. "Porter."

I spend the next half hour talking with Zayna. It is nice to have someone to talk to, but as much as my cousin and his girlfriend might think that they are matchmakers, this isn't going to go any further than maybe friendship. And that's only if I ever see her again

It's getting way too crowded and loud for my liking. Plus I haven't been home too much lately, and I really need to spend some time with my dogs. Trent never lets me use Banjo and Suki as an excuse, so I just tell him I have a long shift at work tomorrow, and he lets me off the hook. It's not a complete lie. I do have a long shift tomorrow, but it's a night shift.

I just want to go home, get into bed, and read with my dogs as my only company. I'm way too peopled out. After some (read: a lot) of pushing from Sloane, I offer to drive

Zayna home on my way. It isn't on my way at all, but she seems to be needing an out as much as I do so I was happy to help. Pretty sure Sloane is hoping that there will be something between us, but it's not going to happen. I'm not looking for anything serious, and Zayna doesn't give the impression that she is either

CHAPTER 4

Torrance

WHEN JONATHAN TALKED me into going out with him and some of his college buddies who were in town tonight, the last person I expected to see was Porter Collins. Of all the people to see out in the wild, why did it have to be him?

Jonathan was the first to notice the large group of professional football players. Not that he's a sports guy, but we went to high school with one of the members of the team, Trent Talbot. Everyone knew Trent in high school; he was a star athlete and had the popularity that went with it. He was a nice enough guy in high school, though we ran in very different circles. Jonathan, Millie, and I were the very definition of choir and theater kids. We lived and breathed it. The only other extracurricular I did was debate. Jonathan and Millie were on the school newspaper. I think I had a couple classes with Trent over the course of high school, but nothing too memorable. It's more I knew of him rather than knew him.

Fast forward to present day, and here we are at a club with a bunch of pro football players who, yes, are objectively attractive. If you're into that sort of thing, which I'm not. I'm basically a monk, or what's the female alternative to a monk? A nun? Is that right? Whatever, I don't do romance, and I certainly would never date an athlete.

That's when I saw him, in the middle of all that testosterone: Porter Collins. Because of course he is. Why wouldn't he be hanging out with football players? That's probably how he meets his dates. He just takes the leftovers. Okay, that was mean. Even I can admit that. That wasn't fair…to the hypothetical women in this scenario I've made up in my head. It was, however, completely warranted for Porter. I mean, look at him now, just sitting there as all those women come over. He's probably just loving all this attention. Don't even get me started on when that blonde was all over him. It's just like in college when he always had girls fawning all over him at every turn.

It's not like I was just watching him all night. I was out with people and having a good time. When I looked back over, the blonde was nowhere in sight, and he was talking with her friend. Last I saw, he was leaving with the friend. How crass is that?!

Jonathan bumps my arm. "What's got you all annoyed?"

"I'm not annoyed," I say defensively. He gives me a look. "What? I'm not!"

"Well, something has your attention, because you've been looking over at where Trent and all his buddies have been all night. And I know you don't have a thing for any of them. Unless your opinion towards football players, or athletes in general, has changed in the last few hours."

"You make it sound like I hate athletes."

"Don't you?"

"No. At least, not all," I admit. "So I didn't have the best experiences in the past with those who chose to participate in organized physical activities…that doesn't mean I don't like them. I just don't have anything in common with them and choose to keep my distance. It's nothing personal."

"That annoyed face looks personal."

"That annoyed face wasn't about an athlete. I recognized someone who was basking in all their glory and taking advantage of it."

Jonathan looks at me, confused. "What on earth are you talking about, Tor?

I sigh. "I saw Porter over there, okay? He just gets under my skin."

"Porter? As in Duncan's friend?"

"The very one."

"You saw Porter, so naturally you decided to sit and watch him all night and stew on how much you dislike how he was out with people who we can only assume are his friends since he was with their group all night?"

"I wasn't watching him all night."

"No. Of course not," Jonathan tries, and fails miserably, to hide a smile.

I point at him accusingly. "Wipe that smile off your face right now."

Jonathan bites down on his bottom lip, but that pesky smile busts out regardless.

"Stop it!" I shove him.

He is full-on laughing now.

"Why are you laughing?" Now I really am annoyed.

"You were jealous," he hiccups between bouts of laughter.

I am completely appalled. "I am a thousand percent certain that I am *not* jealous! How dare you even insinuate that preposterous thought!"

"It's even worse than I thought it was," Jonathan continues to laugh. "Your vernacular gets more complex the more defensive you get."

"I'll show you defensive," I mutter. It's not even a good comeback, but I'm really trying to not say the words that keep streaming through my mind. I made Kiersten a promise that I would stop swearing so much. I tried to slip in some Spanish or French last week. It didn't fly. If she wasn't such a tender heart, I'd say she would grant me a pardon considering the situation I find myself in, but alas, she's too good of a person for that.

I STARE DUMBFOUNDED at Millie and Kiersten. Duncan is actually going to propose. At least, he's getting a ring this time, which is further than he's gotten before. This is the proposal we've been expecting for months, if not years. I mean, they've been together for eight years. But none of that explains why I have to take the ring that Millie snuck out of Amara's room over to Porter's apartment.

"Why do I have to do it?" I demand.

"Because Porter's apartment is on your way to work," Millie reasons. "Kiersten has a test she has to take online, and I have a meeting in the opposite direction."

I eye them both. I won't go as far as to say I don't believe them, but I definitely find it fishy. "Why take the ring to Porter at all? Why not to Duncan?"

Kiersten takes a drink of her orange juice. "Because Duncan said he didn't want to risk losing Amara's jewelry. And he trusts Porter to keep it safe."

I roll my eyes. "So, what, is Porter going to keep the engagement ring too?"

"Probably," Millie and Kiersten both say.

How are they not seeing a problem with this logic? If you claim to be ready for a proposal, marriage, the whole nine yards, then how on earth are you not ready to be in charge of a sterling silver ring that Amara got from Target five years ago?

And this is my biggest issue with Duncan. He's a nice guy, and I know he cares for Amara, but he has zero follow through. If anything seems hard, he just bails. Or makes someone else do the work. And I know it's none of my business, and it's not my life, but it's getting harder and harder to hold my tongue when the subject comes up. And let's just say, as much as the subject of marriage came up before Millie and Mark got married, it's infinitely more now.

"Grumbling isn't going to do anything," Millie says. "The plan has been made; Porter is expecting the ring to be dropped off this morning before he has work."

"Fine. I'll do it. But I don't like it."

Millie pats the top of my head like I'm a puppy. "Good girl."

I mutter under my breath.

"What was that?" Kiersten asks with a raised brow.

I plaster on a fake smile. "I said, can't wait."

"Sure you did."

I grumble the rest of the morning as I get ready for work. I grumble as I get in the car, and I really grumble as I input Porter's address into my GPS. And then I grumble the whole way there. Right before I knock on the door, I put on the best customer service smile I can muster. You know the one.

Porter opens the door, and I'm pretty sure I wasn't who he was expecting. Surprise, surprise. So, when Millie said the plan had been made, obviously some of the details weren't relayed to all parties.

"Torrance," Porter sputters. "I wasn't—"

"Expecting me?" I ask sweetly. "Sorry to disappoint. Aren't you going to ask if I have the goods or something?"

Porter leans against the doorframe and crosses his arms. "You're enjoying this, aren't you?"

I shrug. "It's still early."

There's movement behind Porter, and I see the blonde from the club. Unbelievable. He went home with her friend, and now she's here. He's even more of a player than I suspected.

"Umm, Porter?" The blonde says. She places a hand on his arm. "Sorry to interrupt, but where are the towels?"

Porter looks over at me then clears his throat before turning back towards her. "Second cabinet to the left."

"Thanks." And she's gone.

Porter tentatively looks back at me. Trying to see my reaction? Pretty sure he wouldn't care what I thought. But with how he's watching me, I'm not too sure. "So, do you have the ring?"

"Yeah." I pull the ring out of my pocket and hand it over. "Here. Millie grabbed a ring she doesn't wear too often so there's no rush for Duncan to get it back."

Porter smirks. "I'm guessing you aren't too big of a fan of this whole thing?"

"What, and you are?"

Porter shrugs.

We're in a stand off, and I don't know what to do next. I hear shuffling from inside his apartment and remember the blonde waiting for him inside. With a towel. All thoughts swirling around my brain cease. "Well, I need to get to work. It's a busy day."

Porter pushes away from the doorframe. "Take care, Torrance."

I turn and walk towards the elevator. As soon as I hear the door close behind me, I all but sprint back to my car. I have no idea what just happened. Porter and I had an actual conversation. Sort of. At least there was a moment where we didn't completely despise each other. I don't know what his issue is with me. From the moment that we met back in college, he's always just glared. Not that it bothered me. I'm not everyone's cup of tea, and I'm perfectly okay with that. It didn't take long for me to see him for the player that he was, and I was more than happy to not be his particular cup of tea. In fact, if he likes tea, then I'm coffee.

CHAPTER 5

Porter

I LEAN AGAINST THE door after closing it. I'm not sure what just happened. Torrance and I never talk like that. Ever. It was almost cordial. Why did I lean against the door frame? I have never done anything like that a day in my life. I'm not some suave guy. I do not flirt just to flirt. I especially don't flirt with Torrance.

I feel the hard metal in my hand. Right. She brought the ring over for Duncan to size the engagement ring.

When Duncan told me that one of Amara's roommates was going to drop the ring off at my place, I didn't understand why. I mean, he's the one getting a ring to propose. Why do I need to get roped into this? Why create a middleman? None of it makes sense. I know I should have thought of the possibility, but I really wasn't expecting it to be Torrance who dropped it off. She's hated me from the day we met; there is no way she agreed to that easily.

"What's got you all doe-eyed?" Trent smirks from his stool over by my kitchen island.

I push off the door and roll my eyes at him. "I'm not doe-eyed."

"I'm pretty sure you are. And by the sounds of things, the other voice wasn't repulsed by you."

"Highly doubtful. Torrance hates me."

"That was Torrance?" Sloane asks in an excited voice. Is everything she does always this peppy? She really is the perfect match for my cousin. "She's gorgeous! No wonder you and Zayna didn't hit it off. You already have someone!" She gives a little sigh.

"What are you talking about?"

Sloane looks at me, a little confused. "I was hoping you and Zayna would hit it off the other night, but now I understand why you didn't. You already have someone you're interested in."

"I am not interested in Torrance." Why does everyone keep saying that? I'm not. And I never will be.

"You've had it bad for Tori for years," Trent says unhelpfully.

"Torrance and I have butted heads from the moment we met."

"Butted heads or had explosive chemistry? Because the Tori Rodriguez I knew in high school didn't waste her time arguing with people she deemed unworthy."

"So, with that logic, you get under her skin," Sloane remarks with a dreamy look in her eye that I don't like one bit. "And she clearly gets under yours." She starts clapping and doing the happy giddy squeal as she claps her hands, I'm starting to think this is her natural state. "Oh, it's a clear case of enemies to lovers."

"A case of what now?"

"It's the best trope! But I never thought I'd actually see one in real life."

"This isn't anything like that…trope thing." Whatever a trope is. I'm not going to ask; Sloane would be all too happy to explain.

"It totally is," Trent agrees with Sloane. Not that I should be surprised. She could say that she was only going to eat foods that start with the letter R, and he'd agree with it.

Radishes. Rice. Rutabaga.

Stop it, Porter. Now's not the time to start down a rabbit hole. Your only objective is to stop Trent and Sloane from planning your wedding to a woman whom you can't stand and who equally can't stand you.

"Look, I know you two want me to find someone so that you can drag me into your couple world, but it's not going to happen. And it's certainly not going to happen with Torrance. As I've already stated, she hates me."

"We'll see," Sloane smiles. She leans up to kiss Trent. "I have to get going. I have some filming I need to get done today."

They might annoy me, but I have to admit it would be nice to have someone you care about so completely. I just haven't met anyone that I feel that kind of connection to. Not that I have tried too hard. I don't have time to try. I'm content with my life. I have a career that I love, and I'm working hard to achieve my goals. My life is full. I don't need a relationship to fulfill anything. I have what I need.

♡♡

I FINALLY HAVE my apartment to myself. This shouldn't be a problem when you live alone, but Duncan and Trent have been over a lot lately, and it's draining. They're my best friends, but I also don't live with them for a reason. I like my space, and I haven't had enough of it lately.

Trent is in pre-season training so he's not as busy or traveling, which means he has lots of time on his hands. And bored Trent usually means nothing but grief for me.

Duncan, on the other hand, says he wants to propose to Amara. He says he's ready. He's gotten her roommates involved, but I still don't think it's what he really wants to do. I just feel that if it was something he really wanted, he wouldn't be over here asking my opinion on whether it's a good idea or not. For the record, I think Amara is an amazing person. She has been a great girlfriend to Duncan. She has been nothing but patient with him over the years. I also think that she deserves for him to be completely honest with her. They have been together for almost nine years; maybe it's my own baggage, but I just think that if he was ready to get married, he would have proposed already.

I'm laying out on my couch reading my book, Suki laying down to my left. Banjo is curled up at my feet facing the door; he always prefers to lay on the rug so he can see the door clearly, just in case. I'm a couple chapters in when my phone rings. I know who it is before I look at the screen, because only one person calls me. At least at this time of day. My grandmother.

"Hello?" I say with pretend annoyance. MarMar hates it when I answer the phone this way, so of course it's how I always answer her calls.

"Porter? What's wrong? Why do you sound like that?"

"Sound like what?" I tease.

"Are you messing with me?" I chuckle at her wording. She's been talking with my little sister and cousin. She always tries to use the "hip lingo." Not that I think that is even hip lingo anymore, but what do I know? I'm almost thirty. Half of what my sister says doesn't make sense to me. With eight years between us there is somewhat of a generation gap in what would be considered "hip."

"Yes, I am. I'm sorry. How are you, MarMar?"

She sighs. "Oh, same old, same old. I was just putting a pie in the oven, and I thought I would give you a call. It's been a while since I've heard from you. Wanted to make sure you were still breathing."

"You talked to me last week. Nothing has changed since then. Why don't you tell me why you actually called?"

I know her well enough to know there is an ulterior motive to this call. I talk with her at least once a week, sometimes more. Then there is a hint of panic as I think she might be calling to tell me that something came up in Mom's last scans. Is she calling to tell me Mom's cancer has come back? I take a breath and release it slowly. Surely if the scans came back positive, Mom would have called me as soon as she left the doctor's office. That's our deal. She goes to the doctor and then calls me on the way home so I can explain anything she doesn't understand. And it helps give me peace of mind.

"Trent called me."

A weight of relief settles over me, but it is quickly replaced with a new sense of annoyance towards my cousin. What did he call MarMar about?

"Oh? And what did he have to say?"

"He's worried about you."

I'm sure he is. He wasn't getting anywhere with me in letting him set me up, so he went over my head. Classy move Trent.

"There's nothing to be worried about. Trent is dramatic. You know this."

"He just doesn't want you to be alone. He wants you to be as happy as he is with Sloane. And frankly, I agree. You should be happy."

"I am happy."

"You don't sound happy."

"Well, I am. If you ever learned to do a video chat, I'd show you. I'm smiling right now." I'm not, but it's a lie I'm willing to live with. "Did he tell you I went out with him the other night?"

Most guys wouldn't tell their grandmothers about going out to clubs and being hit on by women, but Trent isn't most guys, and MarMar isn't your average grandmother. She and Grandpa Gentry had their hand in raising all of their grandchildren in one way or another.

The three of us boys are only a few months apart in age, with Nic being the oldest and Trent the youngest, putting me in the middle, with only three months on either side of me. Nic and I were raised more like brothers than cousins since we both grew up at MarMar's house. Trent came to visit most holidays and every summer until we got to high school. Trent saw it as his duty to make sure Nic and I had fun when he was in town. He's always claimed that we are too serious, which may be true, but he's also not serious enough.

Nic and I are both the oldest of our siblings, and Trent is the youngest. We had responsibilities that he never had. His parents might have a dysfunctional relationship, but he has two parents. We don't. We've both taken it upon ourselves to watch out for our younger siblings the best we can.

MarMar clears her throat, bringing me back to the present. "Have you heard a thing I've said? I'd think you hung up, but I can hear you breathing. You're a very loud mouth breather. Did you know that?"

I'm not a mouth breather, but I'm not going to argue with her about it. "Sorry, I got distracted."

"Would this have anything to do with the young lady Trent was telling me about?" There's a hopeful tone in her voice. Sorry to disappoint, MarMar.

"Of course he brought up Zayna. No. She's Sloane's friend. Nothing more. Not my type."

"And what is your type, Porter? Because from what Trent was telling me, it seems your type is feistier than this Zayna."

If it's not Zayna that Trent was talking about then who— Oh, no. He wouldn't.

"MarMar, who did Trent talk to you about?"

I really hope the name I'm pretty sure is about to be spoken isn't the name that is spoken.

"Tori. And I have to say, she sounds delightful." Of course MarMar thinks she sounds delightful. Trent probably described her as some nice person. Which she isn't. At least not to me.

"I have nothing going on with Torrance."

"Torrance? As in the girl you've had a thing for since college?" What is with people?

"I don't have a thing for Torrance!"

"But you did."

"No, I didn't! I never have and never will!"

"Honey, deny it all you want, but how would I even know this girl's name if you hadn't mentioned her over the years? Other than your graduation, I never even saw your campus."

"Everyone keeps saying I talk about her all the time. I don't!" Maybe I complain, but that's it. And it's not like it has been all the time. I haven't even spent that much time around her, especially the last few years since we all moved away from college. Though we did end up moving to the same state and same area. What are the odds of that happening? It's like the universe is against me or something.

"No need to get defensive. I just think you need to keep your mind open. Maybe the reason why she annoys you so much isn't what you think it is. You've always been so guarded. I just don't want you to miss out on something because you're afraid it might turn out like your parents or aunt and uncle." She hit it a little too on the nose.

My mom and dad didn't exactly have the happiest of marriages, with my dad taking off when I was about three. We moved in with MarMar and Grandpa so that they could help take care of me while Mom was at work. Dad would come by from time to time when he was back in town, but it wasn't until I was seven that he told mom he wanted to try again. They had never divorced, though now, as an adult, I wonder why. A year later my sister, Zion, was born. Two years later, Mom was first diagnosed with breast cancer, and we moved back in with MarMar and Grandpa. Dad claimed it was too much for him, and he left again. A few months later, he asked for a divorce.

"Just promise me that you won't keep your guard up forever. You're too special to not share yourself with someone. Maybe it won't be Torrance or Zayna, but someday, someone is going to break through those walls you have built up and is going to see how special my sweet boy is."

"Okay." That's all I can say.

MarMar tells me a couple more things about home and the latest town gossip and then hangs up. Usually when she calls, I feel uplifted and rejuvenated. This time I just feel…alone.

CHAPTER 6

Torrance

J CAN'T GET AWAY from Porter's apartment fast
enough. What on earth was that? In all the years I
have known Porter, we have *never* interacted like that.
Was he flirting? Surely not. That's ridiculous. And what
was with the lean? Who does he think he is, some sort of
romance hero? Because no. Just no.

I get into my Jeep and slam the door. I shuffle through
my phone until I come to my 80s power ballad playlist. I
roll down my windows and blast the music as loud as I can
stand it then put the car into reverse. No better way to clear
my mind than by drowning out my thoughts.

Twenty minutes later, I pulled into my parking spot at
Wade Incorporated. The high rise isn't as intimidating as
it was when I first started, though I would never admit to
ever feeling intimidated by anything. I've very carefully
cultivated the reputation of someone who is confident and
sure of themselves. Never let others see your weaknesses.
I can admit that I come off as abrasive at times, and I'm
certainly not for everyone, but those that care don't matter,

and those that matter don't care. At least that's what my mom always told me when I was younger and would come home upset about something that some girls at school said.

I was lucky when I met Millie and Jonathan. They are two of the nicest and least judgmental people you will ever meet. Jonathan's family had gone through a rough patch, and he had lost a lot of friends due to it. Millie, and her entire family, I hate to call people perfect, but they are basically as close to it as you can get. I mean, I obviously know they have flaws. Millie wasn't exactly forthcoming when she and Jonathan's brother, Mark, started spending time together. Jonathan didn't handle it well when he found out. I found myself in the middle no matter how much I tried not to be. I could see the issue from both sides, and I found them both right in their own way. Thankfully, the two of them can't stay mad at each other for long, and they worked it out. Which is a good thing, since they are in-laws now.

The elevator dings as it reaches my floor. As soon as it opens, I'm off and running. It's a busy day ahead looking at new hire paperwork. Though I didn't start out wanting to work in human resources, it's been a good fit for me. And there are worse things than working for a billion-dollar company right out of college. Though I could do without having to deal with all the complaints about Walter Wade's sons. All three have prominent positions in the company and the attitude that comes with growing up with unlimited amounts of money at their disposal.

"TORRANCE!" I LOOK over to see Will, the club manager at Treble Tone, as I walk through the door. The familiar scent hitting my senses instantly relieves some of the tension from my growing headache. When I'm stressed, I will do one of two things: run or sing. I already ran six miles today so now it's time to sing.

Jonathan and I found this place several months ago when no one else in our friend group wanted to go out. It's now a regular place for me. I'm such a regular that not only do I know employees, but I know other patrons. I basically live in an episode of Cheers when I'm here, only with karaoke. I love the freedom of not knowing anyone outside of these walls; they only know me as the girl who loves to belt Whitney Houston songs, with the occasional Kelly Clarkson or Celine Dion (if I'm feeling extra brave). No one in my regular life, other than Jonathan, knows this place exists. It is my one solace. Something that is completely mine.

"We don't usually see you on a Wednesday."

"It's been a long day." That's an understatement. I had three new hires, four terminations, and a "conversation" with yet another one of Ash Wade's hook-ups. Conquests? However he thinks of them. I'm low enough on the totem pole that I get to deal with all of them. Not that anything ever changes. He's the son of the owner; it's not like he's going to get fired. And he never goes into the realms of harassment. He's at least smart enough in that regard. If only he was more like his brothers and searched outside the employee list for dates.

"What will it be?" Will asks as I slide into a bar stool.

"Where's Angelica tonight?" I look around for the usual bartender.

Will laughs. "It's her day off."

Ah. And I don't usually come in on a weekday so I wouldn't know that. "I guess I'll go with my usual."

"You got it." Will talks to the few other patrons as makes his way towards the stage area. As he makes it up to the stage, he hands a piece of paper to the tech manning the music tonight. It's not who I usually see, so I assume Tony also has the night off.

Will hops up on the stage and picks up the microphone. "How's everyone doing tonight?"

The crowd cheers.

"We've got a great lineup tonight," he looks over at me and winks. "Including a special treat we don't usually get to hear on a weeknight."

Three songs in and I'm questioning if my choice was the right one. This crowd isn't amped up enough for my usual weekend song. I need to change it, but I'm up next. My clothes feel all wrong. They're too loud. They're too much for this group.

I'm really regretting coming here tonight. Why did I come again? Oh, right. Work sucked, and my friends all have their own lives and don't have time for me anymore. Millie is married, Amara is about to be engaged, Kiersten has exams coming up, and Jonathan is doing whatever he does when he's not at work or our house. As for Trina, I haven't spent a whole lot of time with her yet. She's still settling into the house and has family visiting from out of town. Take away my roommates and my childhood best friends, and I have no one. No one outside of my family, anyway, not that my parents are the warm cuddly type. They're more the keep-your-head-down-and-keep-moving-forward type. I am close with my sister, but she lives hours away.

That's it, I'm leaving. I stand up to grab my things right as Will calls my name.

"Up next, we have a real treat for all of you. Torrance Rodriguez with a Whitney Huston classic. Get on up here, Torrance!"

I freeze, but I know what I have to do. I swallow my insecurities and put a smile on my face. I grab the microphone from Will and give him a mock curtsy when he winks at me. The music starts, and it's like putting on your favorite pair of sneakers: everything falls into place. I put all of my frustrations from today, this week, the last couple of months, into my performance. I hit every note. I add in some choreography. It's all second nature by now. The song ends with a standing ovation. I smile, bow, then walk straight back to my seat, grab my bag, and leave. When I finally make my escape, I take in a deep breath of the night air. I'm almost gasping to breathe. I haven't had a panic attack like this since my junior year of college.

I try to find something to focus on, but my mind keeps spiraling. When I finally get my heart rate back under control, I all but run to my car as I see the door to Treble Tone open. The last thing I want is for someone to see me like this. I must always be in control. I don't need anyone. I don't have time or space for weakness.

CHAPTER 7

Porter

DUNCAN IS ACTUALLY going to do it this time. He's actually going to propose. He went and bought the ring yesterday then promptly brought it over here for me to look after. This is further than he has ever gotten before.

"Have you decided when you're going to ask Amara yet?" I ask as I watch Duncan dig through my fridge. Sometimes I swear he doesn't remember we don't live together anymore.

"Not sure yet," Duncan says around a sandwich. "Her parents come into town in a couple of weeks so definitely before then."

"Wouldn't they want to be there?"

Duncan shrugs. "They hate me."

"Wait, you have talked to her parents about this, haven't you?"

I realize I haven't spent too much time contemplating marriage, but isn't it customary for a man to ask permission, or at least let the parents know he's going to ask their daughter to marry him? I know I'm more old school when it comes to the ideas of dating. I was basically raised by my grandparents. I'm not exactly up to speed with what is considered modern-day dating practice. Deep down I'm more of a "country boy" and "southern gentleman" than I will ever openly admit to, but even Trent, the professional athlete who could have any woman he wanted (and did up until he met Sloane), wouldn't ask a woman to marry him without at least telling the parents ahead of time.

"Why would I ask them? There's no way they would agree."

"Isn't Amara close with her family?"

Duncan shrugs again. "They just try and tell her what to do all the time. They never listen to her. They don't care what she wants. They just tell her what they want and expect her to agree."

Guess I hit a sore subject. I know neither of the Doctors Lahiri are the biggest supporters of their daughter's relationship with Duncan. I've only ever met them once, and they were intimidating to say the least.

"I'm sure that whatever you decide, Amara will love it." I might be a skeptic when it comes to love, but I really do want my friend to be happy.

ANYTHING THAT COULD go wrong with this proposal went wrong. Duncan decided that he was going to propose at the beach, which sounds great. He did not, however, plan ahead (not that we are surprised by this) and didn't ensure there was a spot for said proposal. This is Southern California;

all year round is beach weather, so any weekend is going to be overly crowded. Then he gave Amara's roommates the wrong directions to where he was, so Amara ended up being late to her own proposal. In the end, I guess it didn't really matter. Duncan asked Amara to marry him, and she said yes. They're happy. His parents are thrilled. Her parents are, in her words, "processing."

It's been two weeks since the proposal, and I don't know what I was expecting to happen, I guess for Duncan to be over at my place less, not more. He's kind of driving me nuts. Even Suki and Banjo are over all the extra attention he's been giving them, and Suki is never one to turn down extra belly scratches.

"Do you have work tonight?" Duncan sits on my couch scratching Banjo behind his ear.

"Yeah. My usual shift. I need to leave in about an hour. Why?"

"No reason."

I highly doubt that. Duncan knows my schedule. It's been the same for the last several months. If he's asking, then there's something going on. I just don't know if he's going to confess what that is or not.

The look on my face must give away my misgivings because Duncan continues, "Amara's parents are in town, and I was wondering if you were available to have dinner with us, but obviously you aren't since you have work. It's fine."

"Ah. How long are they here for?"

"The week. Apparently, there are some wedding things that Amara's mom wants to check out."

"That's a good sign, isn't it? The fact that they are here to start planning the wedding. It means that they're being supportive."

Duncan shrugs. "Or that they realize that it's happening regardless."

"It's at least a step in the right direction."

"I guess. It makes Amara happy."

I hope for Amara's sake that this is a step in the right direction. She might have started out as my roommate's girlfriend, but I think of her as a friend. Duncan might not think that her parents' approval is important, but I know Amara does.

IT'S BEEN A slow shift, which is just how I like it. Willa's children are visiting, and it's been good to see how much her spirits are lifted having them here. And not just her spirits; the whole floor is lighter and happier than they were before Brody and Bella arrived. They both have their mother's wit and zeal for life. I'm glad that I have been able to have time to sit and get to know them a little better tonight.

"Sorry to interrupt," Carol pokes her head into Willa's room. "Porter, you have visitors."

"Me?" Who would be here to visit me? I look over at Willa. "I guess I better get going." I look at Brody and Bella. "It was nice to finally meet both of you."

"Thank you for everything you have done for our mom! It's been such a relief to know she has someone she can talk to while she's been here," Bella says as she pulls me into a big hug. "Sorry, that probably isn't allowed."

I smile at her. "It's fine. Have a good rest of your night."

I walk out of the room, and I'm met with the last person I was expecting to see tonight, followed closely by his fiancé and soon to be in-laws.

"Duncan, what are you doing here?"

"We were at dinner, and I mentioned that you were working tonight. Doctor Lahiri mentioned that he wouldn't mind seeing the hospital Amara works at, and since you work on a different floor I figured we'd come say hi!"

I look at Amara, and she apologetically mouths, "Sorry."

Her parents roll their eyes as Duncan goes on talking about who knows what. They soon make their way towards Carol's station and are quickly in a conversation with her.

I turn my attention back to Duncan. "Duncan, I really can't just sit and talk right now. I'm at work. I have patients I need to attend to."

"I know. I'm sorry. I just didn't know what to talk to them about at dinner. They were being all doctor-y and talking about their research projects and teaching. Amara was talking about her rotations and what she's thinking about choosing for her specialty, and then when it was mentioned that we were coming here, I just wanted to be able to contribute. I know I shouldn't have interrupted. I just liked them actually taking me seriously for once, you know?"

"It's okay, just don't make it a habit." I know it's rough for him trying to fit in with the Lahiris. I want to be there for him; I'd just prefer if it wasn't at my place of employment.

Thirty minutes later, the whole crew finally leaves. I let out a sigh of relief. I look over at Carol.

"This has got to be the strangest shift I've ever had."

Carol laughs. "That was interesting. I wasn't aware that you knew the illustrious Doctors Lahiri and O'Malley-Lahiri."

"I don't! This is the second time I've ever seen them. I just know their daughter from college."

"Well, they were certainly impressed with all that you do here."

"Is that what you were talking about with them?"

"I just answered the questions they asked, honey."

I laugh. "Sure you did."

As much as Carol can be a strict boss, I know she has a soft spot for me. Not that she would ever admit it.

The rest of my shift, thankfully, is back to normal. No emergencies. No changes for the worse. When I finally make it back home, I'm tired, but after such a slow night I'm feeling a bit stir-crazy. I decide to go for a run before going to bed for a few hours. As much as I'd normally just go to the gym, anything indoors feels too confining.

Three miles later, Suki and Banjo are ready to go back home, but I'm still wound up. I just have so much on my mind. Between worrying about Mom's recent scans, which are thankfully clear, the stress of my PA program, and now this road trip. There is just so much to do, it's a bit overwhelming.

CHAPTER 8

Torrance

$\mathcal{I}$T'S BEEN THREE weeks since Amara and Duncan got engaged, and we finally have time to celebrate. Jonathan was going to make an appearance, but something came up so girls night it is. With the amount of things Millie will probably bring up about married life, I would bet he made up his excuse not to attend. Honestly, I don't blame the guy, I kind of wish I could skip that part of the night as well. Only I wouldn't trade any time I get with Millie these days, so I guess I'll take what I can get. Even the mushy marriage stuff.

"It's been too long since we've done this!" Millie squeals as she curls up on the couch between Amara and Trina. Gosh, I miss having her here all the time.

"Well, someone had to go off and get married and ruin things," I joke, throwing a pillow at her. I'm mostly kidding, but part of me still feels like I'm getting left behind.

Millie is married, Amara engaged. Kiersten has started going out more the last month or so as her class schedule has lightened up. Though she's newer to our group, Trina has become just as much an integral part as the rest of us. It)s almost hard to imagine how we went the last nine years without her with us. But Trina dates. A lot. She has a constant string of new guys in and out the door.

Then there's me. I go to work. I come home. And I run…a lot. Other than my weekly, though it's been more bi-weekly lately, visits to Treble Tone, that's all I do. And even Treble Tone is starting to feel weird. Ever since my panic attack, I haven't been able to really get into it like I used to. I'm always afraid I'll have another attack.

My attacks have majorly lessened the last few years, but this sudden increase is really getting in my head. I've tried all the techniques my old therapist taught me. Nothing is working. So rather than talking things out with anyone, I've started lengthening my runs. I might as well train for a marathon at this point. Or at least talk to my sister about it. She might be younger than me, but that doesn't stop her from trying to mother me from time to time. Probably because she is a mom.

"Tori!" Millie's sing-song voice brings me back to the present. "You good? Felt like we lost you there for a minute."

She's smiling, but her face is laced with worry. It's no secret that I've struggled with anxiety and depression in the past, and I can at times go days without sleeping much, which in turn makes me zone out.

I plaster a smile on my face. "Yeah. I was just thinking about my sister."

That's not a lie, I was. It's where I ended up, anyways. It just might have started off as a spiral.

"How is Carson?" Kiersten asks.

"She's good. Planning Aly's birthday party next month."

"I can't believe she's going to be four!" Millie exclaims. "I feel like she was just born."

"I know. She FaceTimed me last week to show me her new big girl haircut, and I hardly recognized her."

We spend the majority of girls' night catching up on everyone's lives and reminding Millie that as much as we love her attention to details, less is more when it comes to her marriage. We end the night throwing ideas out for Amara and Duncan's wedding. Kiersten is in full planning mode and has magazines thrown all about the living room and two different laptops with Pinterest boards and venue choices pulled up. All the important questions are being asked. What colors does she want? Does she have a particular theme?

As when Millie and Mark got married, Amara isn't having an official maid of honor. It is something we all decided years ago. Since we are all best friends, it just makes sense for us each to take on tasks that go along with our strengths. Unlike Millie and Mark's wedding, Amara is swamped with shifts at the hospital and studying for her boards, plus finalizing what she wants to specialize in, so we each have agreed to take on a little more of the planning to help her out. Obviously, this is her day, and she and Duncan will have the final say, but we are here to help. Millie will take care of food and the cake, Kiersten the flowers and the photographer. Trina is over the bachelorette party and entertainment for the reception, leaving me with dresses and the venue. Millie's mom, Norah, has already volunteered to host a bridal shower and to help with anything else we may need. She is the ultimate party host, after all.

After Amara's parents' last visit, we won't be seeing them much. They have agreed to pay for the wedding but have shown little interest in helping plan it. They will be there to support their daughter, but that's about where it ends. It's okay. We've got this. We've got her.

> **DUNCAN:** Hey, would you have a moment to talk about something I want to do for Amara sometime later today?

> **TORRANCE:** I'll be home around 5:00 if that works.

> **DUNCAN:** Yeah. Amara's shift doesn't end until 7:00 so that works.

In true Duncan fashion, he waiss over an hour late getting to the house. As much as I was annoyed that the later Duncan is, the later it will be before I get to the gym, I know whatever it is he wants to talk about is for Amara. She doesn't have a lot of support about her decision to marry Duncan, and I will not be adding to that stress.

If I've learned anything over the last year, it's that I can be a little overbearing when it comes to my opinions. I'm really trying to change that. Especially when it comes to my friends. They are the most important people in my life aside from my family, and I never want to be the reason why any of them are feeling down.

At 6:15, Duncan finally knocks on the front door.

"Why did you knock?"

Duncan never knocks. He always just walks in. Everyone does. We've always had this kind of open-door policy when it comes to our friends. It might seem unsafe to let multiple people have access to our house, but we live in Ridgeview. Nothing ever happens in Ridgeview. And if anyone ever thought about it, then the high-tech security system that Millie's older brother installed when we first moved into the house would more than protect us. At least it would distract them while we got away.

"It seemed weird to walk in when Amara wasn't here." Duncan's response is surprisingly thoughtful.

"Well, come on in. What did you want to talk to me about? You said something about a surprise for Amara?"

"Yeah! I want to throw an engagement party."

"That's a great idea. But why talk to me about it? Millie and Kiersten are more of the party planners than I am."

Duncan rubs the back of his neck sheepishly. "That's the thing. I want to involve her grandparents, and they can't travel. So it would have to be at their place. And since you used to live with them during college, I figured they would be more receptive if you were to be the one to set it all up."

"You want to plan an engagement party in Tennessee? I mean, I'm sure Oma and Papa O would love to help in any way, but I haven't talked to them since we graduated and they moved to Tennessee to be closer to Amara's aunt and uncle. I don't even have their number."

"I have it! And I'll call them and ask. I just need you to help put it together. Head out a few days earlier to get things set up so we can surprise her."

"How are you going to get her to Tennessee without her suspecting something?"

"Our anniversary is coming up, and we've talked about taking a trip. So, us going to visit her grandparents wouldn't be too far-fetched. I know how much she loves them, and they are pretty much the only members of her family who have been supportive of our engagement, so I also want to show them how much that means to us. This party is kind of a double duty thing. An engagement party for Amara and a 'thank you for all your support' for the O'Malleys."

Duncan is so excited about this, and he seems to have put a lot of thought into it. As much as I know this is going to be a lot of work, it looks like Duncan is getting me with the sympathy card tonight. I can't say no. Duncan has had to deal with a lot of backlash from the future in-laws; he deserves this as much as Amara does.

"Fine. I'll do it. I have some vacation days I need to use. It might be a smaller group since it is out of state, but I'll see what I can do to make this happen."

"Thank you!"

I sigh. Just the thought of a project of this magnitude makes me jittery. I might know Amara's grandparents the best out of our group, but I'm not the party planner or the one you call to make things look right. I'm the one you call on to get the party (that is already planned and set up) started. I'm the hype girl. The first one on the dance floor. This is well out of my wheelhouse.

Guess it's an extra couple of miles tonight then full steam ahead.

"DO YOU HAVE a date yet?" Millie asks as we sit at the dining room table looking over ideas for the engagement party.

"No idea. Duncan was supposed to tell me after he talked with Oma and Papa O, but I'm starting to think I should just call them myself. It's been two weeks, and he hasn't gotten back to me."

"Well, he said around their anniversary, right?"

"Yeah. Have any clue in that pretty little head of yours of when that is? Because I remember them meeting and how she invited him to my birthday party so she could hang out with him outside of class. But then the hanging out just turned into dating."

Millie laughs. "Pretty sure it's the first week of September so that gives you about five weeks."

I groan. I do not even know where to start planning this party. Not only did I get myself roped into planning a party, but it is in a different state. Across the country. I groan again as I start banging my head on the table.

"Come on, no need to be dramatic." Millie pats me on the back.

"I'm not being dramatic," my words muffle as I bury my head under my arms. The coolness of the table is the only relief from the rising panic I'm starting to feel.

"We can figure this out, Tor. You don't have to do this alone."

That's just it. I feel alone not only in planning this party, but in every aspect of my life. I feel stuck. I feel left behind. I feel like everyone is moving on with their lives, and I'm still in the same place I was when all of us moved here after college. Now with these anxiety attacks coming more frequently again, I'm about to my breaking point.

I keep my head down, willing the stinging behind my eyes to dissipate. I will not cry, at least not while Millie is here. She'll worry, and tonight isn't about me, it's about Amara and Duncan.

Once we finally get started planning, we lose track of time. At some point a cork board shows up (I didn't even know we had one), and things start getting pinned to it. Kiersten joins in on the planning when she gets home from work. We're so wrapped up in planning that we don't even notice when Amara walks through the door.

"What are you guys working on?"

All three of us jump at the sound of her voice. We're trying to cover up all of our planning, but it's pointless, and we all know it.

"Nothing," we say in unison.

Amara laughs. "Not suspicious at all."

She walks more fully into the room and looks at all our pins on the boards.

"Aww. Guys, this party is going to be amazing!" She turns to look at us, her cheeks shining with tears. "It really means a lot that you're helping Duncan with this."

"Wait, you know about the party?"

"Of course. Oma called me about it last week. They're so excited."

"Does Duncan know you know about it?"

"No, and none of you better tell him. This surprise party is really important to him, and I don't want to take that away. I know it's been rough on him with how my family has reacted to us getting married, so I want everything to go how he planned."

"And by how he planned, you mean us?"

"Would you trust Duncan to plan a party? I mean, I love the man, but he couldn't plan his way out of a wet paper bag."

"In that case, what do you think about what we have so far?" Millie asks.

"It's perfect."

"I do have one question that will help me in the planning of this whole thing."

Amara looks over at me.

"When is it? And can I have your Oma's number? Duncan never gave me any details."

Amara laughs as she starts tearing up again. "You guys are the best."

CHAPTER 9

Porter

TRENT: How's my favorite cousin?

PORTER: What do you want?

TRENT: Who said I want anything?

PORTER: You only call me your favorite cousin when you want or need something, and since you're a famous NFL player, there's very little that you could need that I can assist you with.

TRENT: You're definitely my most pragmatic cousin.

PORTER: Trent, I have work tonight. I need to be sleeping. What do you want?

TRENT: Okay. Okay. The guys and I are having a get-together this weekend. Do you think I could get Duncan's number? I want to see if he's available to play it.

PORTER: Sure. Not sure if he will be available though. He just got engaged, and she works a lot, so the weekends are really their only time together.

TRENT: He finally took the plunge?! Dude! That's awesome! I'll tell him he can bring her. Heck, he could bring as many people as he wanted. He'd be helping us out of a bind. Doogle was supposed to have a DJ booked weeks ago.

PORTER: Your tight end who just got in trouble for being intoxicated during a game? Not exactly someone I'd put in charge of things.

TRENT: And now you see our problem.

PORTER: Here's his contact info.

TRENT: You're my favorite local cousin.

TRENT: How was that? Does that title work?

PORTER: You're an idiot

TRENT: Love ya, little cuz!

PORTER: I'm older than you, you dweeb.

IT'S SATURDAY MORNING. I should be sleeping. I had a crazy shift last night following a double the day before. The hospital is short-staffed due to a stomach bug that's been going around, and it's been all hands-on deck to help out where needed. I haven't been on my floor all week. I miss my patients. And I really miss my schedule.

I thrive on predictability. Which I know is ironic considering the field I'm in, but I need a predictable schedule. Unpredictable things can happen within my normal construct, and I'm fine. It's when it's all different that I get antsy and anxious. That's probably how I got talked into this brunch with Duncan and Amara. Who does brunch? We're in our twenties, albeit late twenties, but still. Brunch is for people far older than us. Yet here I sit. Eating a mixture of breakfast and lunch foods at a time of day that is neither breakfast nor lunch. What's next? Linner? Lunch and dinner?

Duncan's phone starts to buzz. At first, I think he's going to ignore it, but whomever it is it must be important because he excuses himself from the table. As soon as he is out of earshot, Amara turns to face me.

"Don't tell Duncan I said anything, I'm not supposed to know about it, but he's going to ask you to help with a surprise engagement party he's throwing for us."

"He's throwing himself a surprise engagement party?" I eye her skeptically.

"Not for him, for me."

"How is it a surprise if both of you know it's happening?"

"He doesn't know I know about it. He's not exactly subtle, and he didn't tell my grandparents that it was a secret, so they called me about it. I've known for weeks."

"If he's been planning this for weeks, then why does he need my help?"

"He asked my roommates to help him plan it, but since it's going to be at my grandparents house in Tennessee, they're going to need help getting things there."

"Getting things there? I'm sorry, I'm either tired or dumb because I don't get it. What does any of this have to do with me?"

"Because my roommates have been making centerpieces and decorations. They need to be taken to my grandparents' house. A few of the items are large and heavy so we can't ship them which means someone is going to have to drive them there. Trina can't miss that much work, Millie just got married and doesn't want to be away from Mark that long, Kiersten doesn't do long drives, and Jonathan will have just started the new school year so he can't go. Everyone will be flying in for the party, but that still leaves Tori driving by herself, which none of us like. I've been subtly hinting to him that I don't want her driving by herself across the country. Too many things could go wrong. If he doesn't take the hint soon, I'm going to have to tell him I know about the party and that I need him to ask you to go on this road trip with Tori so that she's not alone."

Amara finally takes a breath. It takes me a minute to process everything.

"So by saying he's going to ask for my help, what you really mean is you're asking for my help."

"Yes."

"And you want me to drive across the country with Torrance, who hates me, by the way, so that she can take items for your surprise engagement party, that isn't actually a surprise but we're pretending it is?"

"See, beauty and brains."

I roll my eyes at her comment. Back in college Amara and I were in the same organic chemistry class, and our professor was constantly going on about how people never took her seriously because she was a woman and that you could be both beautiful and smart. First of all, I agree, a woman who uses her mind is automatically more attractive. Second, it became an on-going joke within our study group.

"And Tori doesn't hate you. She just thinks she does."

"I'm pretty sure she hates me. All she does is glare at me whenever I'm anywhere near her. I don't even know what I did to ignite such hatred."

"I don't know. She's never come out and said why, but you'd have 27 hours and 2,000 miles to figure it out."

"You're not making me want to say yes."

"But you will."

"How are you so sure?"

"Because, despite what Tori tells herself, you're a good guy. And if I had to wager a guess, not knowing why she acts the way she does around you drives you crazy, and given the opportunity you'd love nothing more than to solve the mystery."

I can't even argue with Amara's thought process. I would like to know why Torrance hates me so much. I'd also like to figure out the mystery of what that moment was when she came to my apartment when she brought the ring over. Though I will never admit to any of this out loud.

"Fine, I'll do it. But you better make it abundantly clear that this wasn't my idea. I don't need Torrance mad at me on top of already hating me."

"I completely understand and agree to your terms." Amara sticks her hand out, and we shake on it.

If this is a typical brunch, then I never want to brunch ever again.

CHAPTER 10

Torrance

SOMETIMES I REALLY wonder why I chose this job at Wade. Other than the fact that it will look amazing on my resume and it pays well. Who am I kidding, the pay is the biggest reason why I stay. I wouldn't be making half as much at any other company. It allows me to live completely debt-free, something that I never could have imagined growing up. My parents worked hard and made a lot of sacrifices for our family, including moving our family into a two-bedroom apartment in order for my sister and I to have all the benefits of the best school district in the area.

Unfortunately, all of that extra income comes with a price. Today alone, I had seven interns in my office for various reasons, but ninety percent were related to a Wade offspring. I know I'm the low man on the totem-pole, but when I was assigned to be over new hires and interns, I didn't know that was code for babysitter. I didn't like babysitting when I was younger; the only child I have ever willingly watched is my niece. I definitely don't like babysitting other adults.

I just want to make it through the rest of the day so I can head home, get in my evening run, then get comfy for a night in with my friends. It's movie night, and I have every intention of making all the arguments necessary to get them to watch *Pretty in Pink*. It's been a rough few weeks and I need my Jon Cryer fix!

Four more hours, and then it's all about the Duck Man.

I SHOULD HAVE known something was up the moment I walked in the door. I immediately notice the full smorgasbord of food on the living room table. It is a full-on Gilmore Girls feast that Lorelai and Rory would envy. Pop tarts, popcorn, bowls of candy, tater tots, Thai food. The real give away should have been the fact that *Pretty in Pink* is already up on the screen and queued to start.

"What's going on?"

"Nothing!" Amara answers way too quickly.

"It's girls' night," Millie says smiling.

Okay, they're undoubtedly up to something, and I'm not going to like it. They're baiting me with my favorite things. I know my friends well enough to know when they are buttering me up for something. Amara won't crack. I don't know Trina well enough to know if I can get her talking. Millie will, but it will take too long. I look over to Kiersten. Bingo. Target acquired.

"Why are you looking at me like that?" Kiersten squeaks.

I give her my sweetest smile. "I'm not looking at you in any way."

"Tori!" Millie jumps between me and Kiersten. "No."

She points her finger at me like I'm a puppy.

I grab her wagging finger, feigning innocence. "No, what?"

"Stop going after Kiersten. There isn't anything going on. No one is trying to hide anything from you. "

I study my so-called best friend for a minute. "Nope."

I walk out of the room knowing they will all follow behind me. I wasn't born yesterday. They're going to have to do better than this to pull something on me. Once we make it to the kitchen, I turn to face my now-captive audience.

"I don't believe it. There's junk food, Thai, and the Brat Pack. All things Amara despises. So either one of you did something that I'm not going to like, or one of you is going to ask me to do something I don't want to do."

All four remain silent, but I can feel Kiersten wanting to cave, and Millie is close. Which confirms what I was already feeling.

I turn my attention to Amara. "So, which is it? Millie would have baked enough to feed a small country, Kiersten would have made my bed or done my laundry or something, and Trina doesn't know my idiosyncrasies well enough to use them against me."

"It's nothing." The look on my face must convey that I don't believe her. "It's just everything with the party and you driving all the way to Tennessee by yourself. I don't like the idea of you being alone so I thought it would be nice if you had someone go with you."

"Who are you thinking? Because when we all talked about it, it was abundantly clear that no one was available."

"I thought Porter could go."

"Porter Collins? No! No way! That's the last person on the planet I would want to be stuck in the car with for days on end!"

"He's really a good guy, Tor. I don't know what you have against him, but he really is one of the nicest people I know. And he's Duncan's best friend and the best man. It just makes sense. Besides, he's from Tennessee. He knows the area."

"There's no way he'd agree to this. He can't stand me any more than I can stand him."

"Funny you should say that. He already agreed to go. And his one condition was that you knew that it wasn't his idea."

My brain refuses to even try and comprehend the words coming out of her mouth. Porter Collins, the bane of my existence, not only agreed to go on this road trip but his only condition was that I know it wasn't his idea? What is even happening? First the doorway incident and now this. Porter is becoming a much bigger conundrum than I ever would have imagined.

I look at Amara's expectant face. This party and all of us supporting her and Duncan is so important to her that I know I have to do this. It's just a few days. I can do anything for a few days, even be in a car with Porter for hours on end. It's not like it's going to be 24/7. We have to stop at least a couple times along the way. This isn't going to cause some sort of paradigm shift in either of our feelings towards each other. As much as I hate to admit it, I really wasn't looking forward to being in a car for hours on end with nothing but my own thoughts to keep me company. Even if that means I have to share the space with Beelzebub.

"Fine."

Amara jumps up and down clapping giddily. "Oh yay!"

"But you owe me."

"Anything you want, it's yours."

"Anything?"

"Within reason—I don't like that glint in your eye."

"Don't be scared. It won't be too painful."

"Its the 'too' I'm worried about."

I wrap my arm around her shoulder. "Let's just start with you pressing play on that movie while enjoying a tasty treat."

Amara groans as I lead her towards the couch and the bowl of pure sugary carbs with her name on it.

CHAPTER 11

Porter

*I*T'S BEEN TWO weeks since the now-infamous brunch with Amara and Duncan, and Duncan has yet to ask me "his" favor. Every time I see him, I wonder if today will be the day, or if—more likely—he hasn't picked up on Amara's hints. I've tried really hard not to say anything, since, well, she's not supposed to know anything about us going to Tennessee, but it's getting harder. I need to know more details. Like dates and what all needs to be taken with us. Mostly I need to know how Torrance feels about all of it.

I'd be lying if I said the latter wasn't the biggest of my concerns and what keeps me up at night…or during the day. Since I work at night and sleep during the day? You know what I mean. Torrance is just such a conundrum. Amara wasn't wrong when she said Torrance isn't something I can solve. Lately I seem to have even more questions with zero answers. She's a 7X7 Rubik's cube when I can barely solve a 3X3. It's trying to play three-dimensional chess when the other person is playing Parcheesi.

Since Duncan and Amara finally got engaged, I've seen Torrance way more than usual, which pulls all of these thoughts to the forefront of my mind. From the day we met eight years ago, Torrance Rodriquez has all but hated me, though I guess I can't fully blame her. I didn't exactly give a stellar first impression. In my defense, I had a migraine that day, and Duncan dragged me to a party full of people I didn't know. It was loud, and there were so many lights. There was rollerskating. It's like we were at a twelve-year-old's birthday party. I was over it before I even got there. I should have tried harder to get out of it or left once Duncan and Amara were coupled off, but for some reason I still stayed.

After Duncan left me alone to be with Amara, I made my way to sit near the DJ, which is where I first saw Torrance, dressed in brightly colored sequined shorts, a neon tank top, feather boa, and striped knee socks. Not to mention the metallic roller skates with light up wheels. It was a lot. She was loud and dancing, and it was just more than my head could take.

I asked if she could quiet down.

She said no.

I told her she looked ridiculous.

She called me a moody jackwagon and something in Spanish that I didn't understand, but it doesn't take a genius to know it wasn't a compliment. Torrance stated that it was her birthday, and she would be as loud as she wanted to be. Then turned and skated away.

Later that evening I ran into her, literally. She came out of nowhere when I walked towards the snack bar. I didn't see her until she was on the floor. The whole night was a mess. From then on, every time I was in the same room as Torrance, she glared at me the whole time and went out of her way to be as loud and obnoxious as possible. She's elbowed me a time or two in the stomach when she's been particularly spicy.

I did anything I could to not be in the same room. For the most part, it worked—until junior year when Duncan told me he found the perfect apartment. When we moved in, I learned that Amara and her roommates not only lived on the same floor, but we shared a wall. If that wasn't enough, Torrance and I ended up in two classes together that semester. For one class we were even assigned to the same work group. It was torture. The more we saw each other, the more I became intrigued by her, but I couldn't do anything about it. The damage was done. What was that line from Pride and Prejudice? (My mom and MarMar would watch the miniseries when Mom was in the hospital.) "My good opinion once lost is lost forever." Mr Darcy and Torrance Rodriquez have that in common.

I will admit I was a jerk the first time we met, but we were kids. I'd like to think I've grown up, not that Torrance would give me the time of day or the chance to prove that. There have been moments here and there over the years that seem like she might possibly be starting to see I'm not that twenty-year-old anymore, but they are always short and interrupted.

I have no idea how I'm supposed to survive a roadtrip halfway across the country with her. Especially since it wasn't either one of our ideas.

Best case scenario she accepts my white flag, and we come to a truce. Worst case scenario, she ends me once and for all.

AS SOON AS I get home from my run, my phone dings with a notification.

> **TRENT:** You home?

> **PORTER:** Is this the cousin equivalent of 'You up'?

> **TRENT:** Dude, you're not my type. Besides, Sloane loves when I send her those texts.

> **PORTER:** Gross

> **TRENT:** You started it.

> **TRENT:** So are you home or not?

> **PORTER:** What would you say if I said no?

> **TRENT:** That you were a liar because I saw you get home from your run five minutes ago.

> **PORTER:** If you already knew the answer, then why did you ask?

TRENT: MarMar told me I needed to respect your boundaries.

PORTER: So you chose stalking over invasion?

TRENT: Can we come up or not?

PORTER: We?

I really hope Sloane isn't with Trent right now. Trent invading my space is one thing, but I just got back from my run. I'm sweaty and gross. All I want to do is take a shower. I can't do that if Sloane is here.

TRENT: Ryan's with me. We got done with practice earlier than expected.

PORTER: Come on up.

TRENT: Fair warning, the pipes to the locker room showers burst so we kind of stink. But since you also just finished a workout, I figured you wouldn't mind.

I roll my eyes at the phone. Great, now I can't get right into the shower, and my whole apartment is going to smell like multiple sweaty men. My apologies to Banjo and Suki in advance.

"SO NOW YOU'RE just going to drive all the way to Tennessee with this woman who can't stand you?" Ryan sits on the floor petting Banjo.

I nod.

"You haven't seen her," Trent lifts his eyebrows suggestively. "Tori was hot in high school, but now..."

He lets out a whistle.

I don't know why, but the whole thing bugs me. I know Trent is a good guy, and I know he has a girlfriend who he is devoted to a thousand percent, but objectifying Torrance like that is completely uncalled for.

"Will you stop?"

Trent laughs. "Looks like I've hit a nerve. You seem to have a lot of those when it comes to Tori."

"No. I don't," I reply sternly.

By the look that Trent and Ryan are sharing, they don't believe me.

"There aren't any hidden feelings or thoughts," I clarify. "I just don't like you objectifying anyone based on their looks. You'd think someone who's had to face that on a very public stage would understand."

"He's got you there, buddy," Ryan chuckles. He turns back to face me. "So why do you have to do this road trip to Tennessee? Why can't you just fly?"

I sigh. "Because all of Amara's roommates have been in party planning mode, and there are items that would be too big or too heavy or something to ship. So that means that someone has to drive it all there if it's going to be at the party. And apparently it all needs to be there."

"And," Trent clasps me on the shoulder, "my cousin can't resist helping someone in need."

I shrug out of his grasp. "What's that supposed to mean?"

"That you have a bit of a savior complex. Not in a bad way, but you can't resist helping someone when they ask. Especially if they need it."

"I do not. I'm simply helping because as Duncan's best man it is my job to help with all things wedding."

"And if those wedding things just so happen to help you spend more time with Tori, all the better."

"Will you let it go?" I huff, exasperated. "I do not have, nor have I ever had, a thing for Torrance."

The fact that she's the only woman to intrigue me in the last decade means nothing. Is she attractive? I'd have to be blind not to see it, but I'm not dumb enough to admit any of this to my cousin. He and his big mouth will not only get on my nerves, but somehow word will get back to MarMar, who also seems to think that there is something going on between me and Torrance.

My entire family needs to take a chill pill and just get over the fact that I am single and I like it that way. It's a purposeful choice. Anything they think to the contrary is false.

CHAPTER 12

Torrance

AMARA: Porter was wondering if it would be okay if he messaged you to coordinate travel plans.

TORRANCE: It's not like he has to ask permission. I know he has my number.

AMARA: He was just making sure. Remember, you promised you would be nice.

TORRANCE: I'm always nice.

AMARA: Don't make me switch to video call so you can say that to my face.

TORRANCE: Fine. I'll be nice.

AMARA: In every language, Torrance.

I roll my eyes.

> **TORRANCE:** Fine.

I know I shouldn't be so annoyed that everyone keeps telling me to be nice to Porter. It's not like I can't be nice. I can. I just usually choose not to. It's not my fault. He started it. Which I know isn't very adult of me to say, but something about Porter Collins brings out the child in me. From the moment we met, he's just rubbed me the wrong way. Who knocks someone down and doesn't even apologize? Forget that it was my birthday, it's common courtesy to apologize for something like that.

Porter just has this way of putting me on edge. I feel like he's trying to figure something out, and it's unnerving how he just looks at me like I'm a book he's trying to read. If college is anything to go by, then I'd guess he's trying to figure out why I don't fall all over him. And if I'm being honest, if we would have met under different circumstances, I probably would have been attracted to him. He ruins himself. As soon as he opens that pompous, judgmental mouth of his, he ruins anything his looks have accomplished.

This road trip is going to be a true test of my strength and ability to be the bigger person. I might end up being mute; if you can't say anything nice, don't say anything at all and all that. Or I guess I could just rely on my linguistic skills. If memory serves me correctly, Porter doesn't speak Spanish, and I don't think he went past that one French class we took in college. There has to be some sort of benefit to growing up trilingual.

The biggest scheduling obstacle I'm not sure how to work around is how I'm going to get to my niece's birthday party and back so that we don't get too far behind on getting to Nashville. We only have a week to get to Tennessee before the party. But I can't miss Aly's birthday. My parents already won't be there due to a work conflict, so I have to be there, for Aly and for Carson. Our parents try to be supportive, but it's been rough. They love Aly, but I would be lying if I didn't say I thought they could do more. Carson moved in with our grandma, with whom they have had a strained relationship, when she was pregnant, but Carson is still their daughter. And it's not like Valley Creek is that far away. It's only four hours. They could make a day trip and see them. But instead of doing that, they only see Carson in person when she makes the drive to Ridgeview. I get that they work, and they work hard, but not so hard that they don't take weekend trips or vacations to all over. It's a constant argument I have with my parents.

I make it a point to go see Carson and Aly as much as I can on top of FaceTiming at least once a week. Usually more. Carson and I are constantly texting, and I message Aly on her tablet daily. I want them to know that I'm always there for them. No matter what. So being at this birthday party is vital for me and my little sister.

> **PORTER:** Hey, Torrance, it's Porter. I just wanted to touch base about Tennessee. The itinerary, when you want to leave. What's the ETA? What all we need to bring with us, and so on. I have work tonight, so

I might not respond right away. Just let me know your thoughts.

TORRANCE: I'll send a list of what needs to be taken. As far as the timeline, I have my niece's birthday party the weekend before, so I'll have to drive there and back before we go. We need to leave no later than Sunday afternoon if we want to have plenty of time to get to Nashville before the party on Sunday.

PORTER: Okay, where is your niece's birthday party?

TORRANCE: Valley Creek

PORTER: I just put that into my GPS, and that's four hours away! Are you really going to go there and back just to head back that way? When is her party?

TORRANCE: Saturday. . .

PORTER: So, you plan on going to a birthday party on Saturday. It's family, so I'd assume you'd stay the night then get up to drive back to Ridgeview just to get back into the car? Why don't we just leave when you were planning on going to Valley Creek and then leave from there?

PORTER: And before you freak out about me inviting myself to your family event,

I already looked up a couple of BnBs in town, and they have room. I'll just hang out in town while you have family time, and then when you're ready to head out, we will already be four hours closer.

TORRANCE: That's surprisingly thoughtful of you. Are you sure?

PORTER: You make it sound like I'm a jerk.

PORTER: Don't answer that.

I can't help the smile that spreads across my face as I read that last text message. I don't know who this thoughtful guy is, but it's not the guy that I've known the last eight years.

TORRANCE: Are you sure? I was thinking of leaving Thursday after work. I know you work so I wouldn't want to put you out. And there isn't exactly a whole lot to do in Valley Creek. You'd get bored.

PORTER: Don't worry about me. I already switched things around so my last day of work is that Wednesday. I wanted more than enough time to get everything settled with my dogsitter.

TORRANCE: If you're sure? Then I accept.

Amy Green

PORTER: Did you just agree to something I suggested?

TORRANCE: Don't let it go to your head. I'm still not going to make this road trip easy.

PORTER: I wouldn't expect anything else.

PORTER: Oh, I forgot to mention that Trent said I could borrow his SUV so we would have more space with all the stuff we need to bring.

TORRANCE: Trent?

PORTER: Trent Talbot? My cousin? You went to high school together?

TORRANCE: I keep forgetting you're related to Trent.

TORRANCE: I was planning on taking my Jeep, but it would be pretty cozy with both of us, our stuff, and the stuff for the party.

PORTER: So I can tell him yes?

TORRANCE: Fine.

PORTER: Wow, you agreed to two things in one conversation. Are we starting to get along?

TORRANCE: Don't push it. Think of it as a truce to make this trip bearable.

PORTER: Fair.

TORRANCE: I'm making a road trip playlist. What kind of music do you like?

PORTER: Whatever you want. I'm not too picky.

TORRANCE: I highly doubt that.

PORTER: I don't really listen to music.

TORRANCE: That's a travesty if ever I heard one.

PORTER: I mostly listen to audiobooks.

TORRANCE: Let me guess, self-help?

PORTER: Biographies, if you must know.

TORRANCE: You're even more of a nerd than I thought!

TORRANCE: Promise me no audiobooks will make an appearance while we are in the car.

PORTER: Fine. But you need to promise me that there are no show tunes. I've heard stories of trips you roommates have taken.

TORRANCE: Deal. That's more Millie's thing anyway.

I just had a civil and cordial conversation with Porter. And I enjoyed it. What is happening? I mean I know it was just text messages, and we weren't in the same room, but could this mean we might actually get along on this road trip? Because that would be unexpected, but it would also make the trip a whole lot easier.

"What's got you so smiley?" Kiersten asks, walking into the living room.

I hadn't even realized I was still smiling. *What is going on?*

"Just talking with my sister." It's a bold-faced lie, but no need to have anyone reading into anything. Especially since I have no idea what else I could say that wouldn't lead to more questions than I have answers.

"Is she excited about you coming next weekend?"

"Yeah!" My voice cracks. I should probably call her and tell her that Porter is coming. Even if he will be staying in town. It's better to get her inquest out now before I show up with a man at her doorstep. Then she can help me prep our grandmother because there is no way that Bonnie would let Porter drop me off and not make a scene. The best chance I have is to get Carson on my side.

♡♡

THIS TRIP HAS really snuck up on me. I keep making sure I have everything ready to go. Decorations? Check. Party favors? Check. Contact info and flight information for Duncan and Amara? Check and check. Not to mention making sure I have everything I need for myself for this trip. Have I mentioned how out of my depth I am at all of this? At least it will all be over soon, and I will be able to leave all future planning and preparation to the (almost) professionals. I have to admit I'm surprisingly not dreading traveling with Porter. We've had multiple text conversations this week, and we've gotten along every time. That's never happened before.

I'm mostly nervous about our stop in Valley Creek. Carson all but laughed when I told her Porter was coming. She insisted that Bonnie was going to invite him to stay at the house rather than the BnB. I argued, but I also know that it is a very strong possibility. And if she does, she will win. No one argues with Bonnie and wins. She is one stubborn woman. Wonder where I get it from?

Porter is supposed to be here in thirty minutes, so I go through this ridiculous checklist that Millie helped me make all over again. It's a nervous tick at this point. The last thing I want is for us to forget something. I guess at this point if we forget anything, we either get it when we get there or we go without it.

I have been jittery all morning; I even beat my personal best mile time when I went for my run this morning. I feel like I've eaten a handful of those chocolate covered espresso beans when I haven't had a drop of caffeine.

"I forgot how fidgety you get before a trip," Millie says, making me jump. I didn't hear her come in. I didn't even know she was here.

"Geez! You scared me!"

"Sorry," she apologizes.

"What are you doing here? Shouldn't you have work?"

Millie shrugs. Knowing her, she's taken it upon herself to babysit me. Without Amara and Kiersten here, she's probably thinking I'll make a scene when Porter gets here. Well, joke's on her.

"When's Porter supposed to get here?" Millie says in a tone so casual, it's suspicious. Millie doesn't do casual. She wears all of her thoughts on her sleeve and right now her thoughts are screaming she doesn't trust me to be nice.

"He'll be here shortly. I wasn't aware the two of you were such buddies."

"I wouldn't say we're buddies. I mean, I know him. Obviously." She's fidgety and talking fast.

She definitely is on babysitting duty. And I'd bet double or nothing she put herself up to it. Amara is trying to stay as out of this as possible so she's not completely lying to Duncan, and Kiersten knows better than to try and get me to behave a certain way. One would think my best friend since we were twelve would know this as well, but then she wouldn't be Millie. Part of me wishes she had a baby just so she would stop mothering the rest of us. Not that I'm ready for any of my friends to become a parent, but then I wasn't ready for her to get married either, yet here we are.

Now not only do I need to shake off the apprehensive thoughts I'm having about this trip, but I need to try to prevent a spiral that could lead to a possible anxiety attack.

I make an excuse to go back to my room so I can clear my head. A few stretches and jogging in place helps ground me enough that I can refocus on the task at hand. One more deep breath, and I'm as ready as I can be for Porter to get here so we can get going.

CHAPTER 13

Porter

A S I PULL into Torrance's driveway, she all but bolts out the door.

"Oh, good, you're here! Let's get the show on the road!"

"Either you're really excited to get to Valley Creek, or something is up."

"Let's go with the first one," she says as she shoves me towards the open garage. "We should start loading these boxes—we have a long drive ahead of us."

I look at my watch. I'm fifteen minutes earlier than we had discussed, which was already an hour earlier than we had originally planned. When Torrance texted earlier this morning, she asked if I'd be ready to go a little earlier than we had talked about. At first, I thought she was just excited to see her family, but now I'm wondering if there was something else to it.

"Are you sure you're okay?"

"Yeah," she squeaks then clears her throat. "Why wouldn't I be?"

"Well, you asked to leave an hour early, and now you're all but shoving me into the garage so we can pack the boxes into the back of the car."

Torrance lets out a long sigh. "Everyone has been driving me nuts, and I already get a little anxious before starting a trip, and I've double, tripled, even quadruple checked that I have everything ready to go so everyone asking me if I'm okay just sets me more on edge. It's like no one trusts me to have things together or something."

"I'm sorry. I didn't mean to start anything."

Her head shoots up as she meets my eye, a confused look on her face. "I didn't say anything about you. Honestly, you're the first person to talk to me normally all week."

"Sorry, I just assumed. You have to admit in the past you would have insinuated that it was at least in part my fault."

"I really have been a brat all these years, haven't I?"

I don't answer. We've been getting along the last few days in our text messages, but now that we are in person I'm not sure what might set her off. We called a truce, but actually being in a truce is a different story.

"Your lack of response, while wise, also tells a whole lot about my behavior. I'm sorry. I know I can't change the past, but I did promise a truce this trip, and I am a woman of my word."

"I believe you."

"Do you?"

"I'm here, aren't I?"

She smiles, and it's a sight to be seen. I don't think I've ever seen her smile, at least not directed towards me. It makes my brain synapses go a little haywire. If I'm not careful, I might start to think Torrance is pleasant to be around.

I clear my throat. "We should get these boxes in the back of the Escalade."

Torrance snorts. "Trent would have a flashy Escalade."

"Just be glad we have his black one. He could have suggested we take his girlfriend's."

Torrance quirks her eyebrow.

"It's pink. With a light blue interior."

"Who's Trent dating, Barbie?"

I laugh. "You're not too far off."

"I wasn't aware they made pink cars. At least not outside of Mary Kay employees."

"He had it customized for her birthday a few months ago. Apparently, Sloane has always dreamed of driving a car like she had for her Barbies growing up."

"And the human equivalent to a Ken doll would be more than happy to make that happen."

"Yep."

"Well, I'm glad we will be driving Trent's plain black one then."

We finally get the last of the boxes in the back, and then I load Torrance's luggage in the backseat with mine. I figured it would be easier to get our personal things in and out of the car if they weren't mixed in with the boxes since we don't need those until we get to Tennessee.

I knew Millie was here, though past a greeting when I first arrived, she has mostly stayed out of our way as we packed up the car. She goes to give Torrance a big hug and hands her a large bag. I have no idea what could possibly be in it, but Torrance laughs and puts it by her feet in the passenger seat. I guess I'll find out what that is at one time or another.

I wasn't expecting Millie to come over to my side of the car with another large bag.

"What is this?" I ask as I take the bag, which is strangely heavy.

"It's a little something I put together to help you on your road trip."

I eye her waiting for an explanation.

"Everything you need to know about traveling with Torrance is in there. She is one of my best friends, but she's rough to travel with." Oh, great. "Follow those instructions," she points to the bag, "and you might just survive."

"Uh, thanks?"

Millie smiles. "Have fun!"

I put the bag in the backseat. I will look at what that was all about later.

I get into the driver's seat and look over at Torrance. "Ready?"

"Not even a little bit, but let's go."

I turn the key in the ignition and pull out of the driveway. It is quiet for a few blocks before Torrance speaks.

"Are we just going to drive in silence, or can I turn on the radio?"

"The radio is on." I point to the console that clearly shows that music is playing. "I just had it turned down when I was pulling into your house since I was on the phone. Go ahead and turn it up."

I check my mirrors and start to make my way into the next lane. This Escalade is a much larger vehicle than I'm used to driving. I'm grateful Trent loaned it to me, but why does he have to drive a yacht? I know he's a big guy, but he's not that much bigger than I am. I fit in my Camry just fine. Besides, I know full well that his other car is a Mustang.

"This is the music you were listening to?" Torrance sounds almost appalled.

"What? You said no audiobooks." I shrug. "What's wrong with Hootie and the Blowfish?"

"Nothing…if you're our parents." Torrance throws up her hands. "You know what, no. Not even okay for them."

She's silent for a long beat. I take the freeway onramp heading east. According to my GPS, we should make it to Valley Creek in about 4 hours and 35 minutes. I can't believe she was planning on making this drive twice. I do feel a little guilty for basically inviting myself to come along to a family function, but I already contacted the BnB in Valley Creek and have a room for the next two nights. That way Torrance can have her family time before we head out Sunday afternoon. I'll explore what there is to see in Valley Creek, and then I'll study. I planned for downtime and brought my textbooks with me. I won't be in her hair at all.

Torrance searches the radio stations for something she deems worthy of listening to, and the huffs of frustration are rather amusing. Every time I make a comment about how a particular song that comes on isn't so bad, she just glares at me like I've grown three heads. Apparently in this analogy I become a hydra from Greek mythology. See, I read more than biographies. I also listen to lectures on Greek mythology in my spare time. Yeah, I hear it too. I really am a giant nerd.

"There are no good stations!" Torrance rants. "What are people supposed to listen to while they're in the car? And what's with all the commercials?"

"I thought you were making a playlist?"

Torrance rolls her eyes at me. "I did, but I was planning on using those for when we didn't have clear radio service."

"You made more than one?" I arch my eyebrow.

Torrance sighs exasperatedly like it's the most obvious thing in the world. She must have been a bundle of fun as a teenager. "I made one for each day, if you must know."

"But you didn't make one for today?"

"No," Torrance growls. "Usually when I drive to Valley Creek I just listen to the radio. But the radio doesn't usually suck this bad!"

I'm really trying to tread lightly here. We've gotten along so far, but this little tantrum is getting out of hand, and over what? The radio not having music that she currently wants to hear? I look at the clock. It's only been forty minutes since we left Ridgeview, but I'm going to snap if she keeps this up. We promised a truce, and I mean to keep up my end of the bargain, but I can't take any more complaining about something so trivial.

"Have you eaten?"

"What's that supposed to mean?" Torrance snaps.

I take in a deep breath to calm my ever-growing nerves. My left eye feels like it is about to start twitching.

"Nothing," I grit out. "I was just going to say, since we left earlier than planned, I didn't eat when I planned to, so if you were hungry, I was going to suggest we stop and eat. That way we won't get stuck in as much traffic. If you aren't hungry, then I will just get a protein bar out of my bag."

"I could eat," Torrance mumbles.

"What was that?" I ask as if I didn't hear her clearly the first time.

Torrance doesn't even try to hide her annoyance. She knows I heard her just fine. I guess so much for our truce. Not even an hour in and we are already heading towards our usual bickering. Guess we really do only get along in text messages.

"I could eat," she over-enunciates.

"Where do you want to eat?" Apparently, it's the wrong question.

Torrance throws up her hands. "I don't care, Porter! This was your idea!"

"Are you PMSing or something? Because geez!" As soon as the words are out of my mouth, I regret them. I don't know what came over me. I have never once said anything like that to anyone. Not even my sister or cousin who is basically like a sister to me.

Torrance's eyes widen and her face reddens. "I can't believe you would ask me that! You as— "

"I know!" I interrupt. "Sorry! I don't know what came over me." I try to lower my voice and even my tone. "That was completely uncalled for. I have never said anything like that before, and I have no idea where it came from. I guess I'm hangrier than I thought." I point to a sign with a list of places coming up. "Looks like there is a Denny's coming up. Are you okay with that?"

"Sure."

"There's a gas station right next to it so we can go ahead and top off the tank while we're stopped."

"We've driven maybe fifty miles, and you want to top off the tank already?"

I swallow my annoyance and plaster a smile on my face that I really hope doesn't look like the Joker. "I just thought that it wouldn't be a bad idea since we were already stopped next to one. If you would rather, we can just stop later when we need to."

"No, it's fine. I was just trying to figure out if you were a fill up every half a tank kind of person."

"No. I fill up at a quarter of a tank like a normal person."

Torrance scoffs. "Like a normal person? You mean like a grandpa."

"And when, pray tell, do you fill your tank? When the light goes on?"

Torrance waves me off. "Everyone knows you have a good twenty miles after the light comes on."

I can feel my eyes bug out of my head. She has to be joking. "Don't you worry about getting stranded somewhere?"

She shrugs. "Hasn't happened yet. Besides, that's what AAA is for."

"No, AAA is for roadside assistance like a flat tire, not because you were too shortsighted to fill up your gas tank."

"You might think I'm shortsighted, but I'm not the one who's going to miss his exit." Torrance points to the exit right as we pass it.

I blow out a breath. "You couldn't have said something earlier?"

"Why would I? I'm shortsighted, remember?"

This woman is going to be the death of me! We haven't even made it to our first stop, and I'm contemplating ways I could get away with leaving her behind, but then I remember why I'm here, and I stop those thoughts in their tracks.

I get off on the next exit. It takes a couple more turns since we have to backtrack a little, but I finally pull into the Denny's. Before I turn off the car, I turn to face Torrance.

"Look, I know I'm the last person you want to be on this road trip with. And I'm sorry, but can we call another truce? It's already going to be a long trip, and it's just going to be that much longer if we are bickering the whole time."

Torrance snickers as she says "bickering" under her breath. I eye her. At a normal volume, she says, "Sorry."

"Let's just get something to eat." I turn off the car and get out. I hear Torrance's door as she slams it behind her.

We take seats at the counter and order our food. Eating in relative silence is much less awkward sitting at the counter than in a booth, so good call there. Pretty sure we both need a break from each other. When we get back in the car, I do not get gas. No need to start that argument all over again. Torrance finally finds a radio station that she can deal with, and we drive without saying a word for a good two hours.

The silence is only broken when I take the next curve a little sharper than I need to.

"Slow down, you maniac!" Torrance yells. "This isn't *The Fast and the Furious*! And you are not Paul Walker!" Under her breath she mutters, "May he rest in peace."

"Chill out!" I bark back. "It was a sharper curve than it looked."

"Well, maybe if you weren't driving like you were in the Indy 500 you would have seen the curve for what it was!" She snaps back.

While she's lecturing me on proper driving etiquette and speed control, I take the next curve even harder. Because I can. And because I know it will really annoy her.

She slugs me in the arm, making me jerk the wheel.

"What was that for?"

"You're doing it on purpose!"

"You hitting me in the arm that is holding the steering wheel isn't helping matters!"

"Then stop," she huffs while crossing her arms and glaring out the window.

"Stop hitting me," I retort.

"It was once, you big baby."

"I think I preferred when you weren't talking to me."

"Fine by me."

"Fine."

"Fine."

I laugh, "You just have to have the last word, don't you?"

Miss High and Mighty opens her mouth to speak but stops herself just to prove that I'm wrong, all while proving me right. This stupid road trip can't end soon enough.

CHAPTER 14

Torrance

'VE NEVER BEEN so happy to see the sign for Valley Creek in my life. I love my sister, and I love coming to visit her, but Valley Creek? Not so much. I really don't understand what she loves so much about this teeny tiny town. Other than the fact that they welcomed her with open arms when she moved here, eighteen, divorced, and pregnant. Okay, so maybe I can see why she loves it here. But still, it's just so small! Population: 847. Our high school was bigger than that. Heck, my graduating class was three-fourths the size of this town.

"So, this is Valley Creek."

I look over at Porter, interested in what this desolate place looks like from his point of view. I've been coming here to visit my grandmother since long before my sister moved here so I don't remember what it was like the first time. He's too hard to read, not that I've ever taken the time to try before.

It's the first either of us have spoken in over an hour, and as much as I hate to admit it, I kind of wished we would have talked more. Not that I want to talk to Porter, but it would have made the drive go by a whole lot faster. I don't do silence well. I could only text so much since I didn't want to kill my battery. I'm sure this fancy car has plenty of spots for me to plug my cord in, but it's all the way in the back seat, and I wasn't about to ask Porter to pull over so I could grab it. Nope. I just sat in the front seat and pouted like a child. Not exactly the most stellar start to our trip. It's going to be a long week. At least I get to see my sister tonight. She will give me some much-needed perspective. And grief, but mostly perspective.

"Yep. In all it's glory."

"How did your sister end up living here?"

"She moved in with our grandmother after her divorce was final."

"Well, that's nice that your grandmother was able to be there for her. I was basically raised by my grandparents, so I get it."

"You were raised by your grandparents?"

"Yeah, well, and my mom. But she was sick a lot, so they helped out a lot."

"Where was your dad? I'm sorry. That's a personal question. You don't have to answer that."

"No, it's fine. My dad wasn't around much. He took off when I was little, came back into town on and off. He finally took off for good when my sister was a baby."

"That must have been hard. I'm sorry."

Porter shrugs. "I don't really have any thoughts about it. He was hardly around. Once he finally signed the divorce papers, it was more like a relief."

"That's a lot to deal with as a kid. My parents are far from perfect, but they always were there when we needed them. At least for the big things." Most of the time, anyway. But Porter doesn't need to know all the Rodriquez family drama or all the nitty gritty details of my childhood. It's not like my parents didn't care or abandoned me like his dad did. They just worked a lot. They sacrificed a lot for us, but they also chose to do things that took them away from home a lot. Then once they were "empty nesters," they took that literally.

"I'd guess it's not much different than what your niece has to deal with. Divorce has its ups and downs, but it's still hard when you've a young kid."

"Aly never knew her dad. My sister didn't find out she was pregnant until after the divorce." I look over at Porter who is clearly holding back his thoughts on the subject. "And before you can ask, yes, Carson told him. He just wasn't interested in being involved."

"Sounds like a real winner."

"You have no idea."

"It looks like the GPS is taking me to the center of town. Where is your sister's place?"

I give Porter directions to the house. As soon as we turn onto the street, all of my fears are confirmed. It's a whole welcoming party. Carson, Aly, Bonnie, their neighbor Luella, and Carson's friend Jasper. Oh, goody.

"I'm guessing it's the house with all the waving people in front of it?" Porter unsuccessfully tries to hold back a laugh.

"What gave it away?" I deadpan.

Porter parks the car, and I jump out just in time to catch Aly as she launches into my arms.

"Oreo!"

"Kitty Kat!"

I squeeze her as I start to spin, not stopping until I'm dizzy. We're both laughing. Carson swoops in next, giving me a bone-crushing hug. It's been too long since I've seen her.

"You're making it hard to breathe," I wheeze.

"Sorry." She lets go, but leans in as she whispers, "That's Porter?"

I roll my eyes. "Yep."

"He's cute."

I hip check her. "Stop it."

"What? He is. Are you sure there isn't anything going on there? Because dang, Tor."

"Stop, before Bonnie hears you. The last thing I need is her getting ideas."

"Let her get ideas. I'm so tired of her constantly asking me if there is anything going on with me and Jasper. We're friends. That's it, but she just can't let it go."

There's so much I could say about all of that, but I just got here, and if I'm not careful, Bonnie is going to invite Porter to stay here, and that is the last thing either of us want. If that car ride from Ridgeview is any indication of how this road trip is going to go, then the next couple of days are going to be a much-needed oasis.

Carson starts to giggle.

I eye her suspiciously.

"If you're worried about Bonnie asking Porter to stay, then you might be too late." She points over to where Bonnie has clearly zeroed in on Porter as he and Jasper unload my bags.

I mutter a swear under my breath.

"Shh. Aly will hear you."

"Sorry."

Carson starts to giggle again. "Oh, this is going to be more fun than I thought it would."

I glare at her. "Why do you say that?"

"Because he clearly gets under your skin. And I kind of like seeing you get all flustered about a man."

"I am not flustered!"

"Oh, you so are! You like him."

"No, I don't!"

"You like him a lot!"

I unlatch my sister's arm from around my waist.

"I'm walking away from you now!" I say, giving her a parting gesture behind my back as I walk towards Bonnie and Porter.

"Bonjour, Mamie," I greet my grandmother.

My grandmother's eyes glisten with tears as she pulls me into an all-encompassing embrace.

"Ma douce fille," she says in French as she kisses both of my cheeks. It's been this way since we were kids, Bonnie will speak in English, but only if she has to. If you speak French, she will speak to you in French, especially if she wants to have a private conversation in front of people. "I was just talking to your handsome young man."

I really am hoping Porter never learned French. I'm really putting all my eggs in the basket that he gave up after that one semester of college, because I have a feeling Bonnie is only going to get more embarrassing.

"He's not my young man."

"He could be," she pats my cheek. "You are too picky."

"I'm not too picky. Besides, I'm not looking."

"Then open up your eyes! That boy is magnifique," Bonnie argues as she switches back to her more usual mix of English and French.

"Mamie!" I shush her. "He'll hear you!"

"And what's so bad about that?"

"Because we aren't dating. We aren't even friends. We're just…" I don't even know how to explain what we are. Two people who have mutual friends who can at best sometimes tolerate one another.

"Stubborn, stubborn girl."

"I wonder where I get that from?" I ask, giving her an exaggerated eye roll.

"I like to blame your father."

And that's my cue to drop the subject. It's no secret that Bonnie doesn't exactly like my dad. Well, it's more that she doesn't like my abuela. And doesn't like that when Abuela moved in with us when I was a kid, we spent less and less time with Bonnie. When it came down to choosing which side of the family we would spend holidays with, it was always Dad's and hardly Mom's, which I know hurt Bonnie's feelings. It didn't help that the few times we did go to spend Christmas or Easter with Bonnie, my abuela would refuse to come and then would pull out all the stops to make my dad feel guilty about leaving her behind, which usually ended up with us cutting our trips short. During one particular visit when I was in high school, words were exchanged between my parents and Bonnie, and that was that. They've hardly spoken since.

"Porter, I know you have a reservation at the BnB in town, but you should really stay for dinner," my sister says.

I try to catch her eye, but she's a professional avoider. "Ms. Luella made her famous bread pudding, and Bonnie made a roast that smells absolutely divine."

"Oh yes, Porter! Please stay! Our food will be much better than anything you will get in town," my grandmother says in her thick French accent.

I hear Jasper snort as he tries to hold in a laugh. It doesn't get past Bonnie's attention either. "Not a peep out of you, Jasper. You know I'm right. I'm the best cook in the county, and the only one close is Luella."

"I would never argue that, Bonnie." Jasper looks at my grandmother lovingly. I'm glad he's here for my family, even if my sister is a big dope and doesn't realize what's right in front of her face.

"It would be an honor," Porter says, then turns to look at me. "If that's okay with you?"

Before I can answer, Carson jumps in. "Of course it's okay! The more, the merrier!"

I look over at him and shrug. "If you're sure you can handle it. I know you were looking forward to your quiet time."

Porter's eyes narrow. "You know, I had a lot of quiet time in the car. I think I can handle some talking."

"You were in a car with Tori for over four hours and you had quiet? Was she sleeping or something?" There goes Carson being all little sister-y again.

"I can be quiet," I argue.

"Not usually by choice." Her gaze goes back and forth between me and Porter. "Oh, I get it. You were in one of those arguments I've heard all about."

I glare at my sister, hoping she understands everything I'm not saying. By the look of amusement on her face, she knows exactly what I'm saying. She's just not listening.

"Will you stop?" I grit out, switching into Spanish.

"Stop what?" Her tone is innocent, but her face looks like a cat who caught a canary. "He's cute, and you know it."

"I never said he wasn't."

"So you admit it?" Carson asks triumphantly.

Before I can answer, Bonnie breaks in. "No more Spanish! No one can understand what you are saying when you speak in that terrible language."

Kind of the point, Bonnie.

"Sorry, Mamie."

Bonnie turns her attention back to Porter. "I'm sorry about my rude granddaughters. You were saying you will stay, yes?"

Porter swallows back a laugh. "Yes, Mrs. Lemaire, I would love to stay for dinner."

Bonnie blushes—she blushes! The woman is harder than a walnut, and she blushes at Porter saying her name? What is going on?

"Call me Bonnie, all the kids do."

"Well, then, Bonnie, it's a pleasure."

CHAPTER 15

Porter

TORRANCE'S GRANDMOTHER IS one persuasive woman. Not only did she get me to stay for dinner, she insisted I stay for dessert because "you can't have a meal that doesn't end with something sweet." All of that after courses of an appetizer, soup, fish, salad, the roast and potatoes with glazed carrots, and cheese. I don't think I have eaten so much in my entire life. And everyone else just sat around the table like it was normal.

After we finally finished eating, Aly asked if we could play dominos. Kind of a random game for a four-year-old to want to play, but who am I to judge? She schooled me. Hard.

Everyone sat around talking and laughing. It was hard not to notice anytime Torrance and her sister wanted to talk without anyone else knowing what they were saying they would switch to Spanish. Bonnie would scold them in a mixture of English and French. I'm just going to keep it to myself that I understood everything they were saying. Partly because I'm scared of what Torrance might do to me if she knew I not only was at least partly listening to her conversation but also understood it. I'm just going to keep the knowledge that she does in fact think I'm attractive to myself.

After a full evening of food and visiting, Jasper walked Ms. Luella home then headed home himself.

I tried to make a graceful exit, but I was outnumbered and outwitted by three-fourths of the Lamaire/Rodriquez women. So I am now carrying my things up to the guest room rather than staying in the BnB. When I told Bonnie that I needed to at least call and cancel my reservation, she just waved me off. I'd look them up online, but Bonnie doesn't have WiFi, and my phone is having a hard time getting anything to pull up on LTE. All I can do is call or text. Nothing else works. I don't understand how my GPS worked just fine getting into town, but after driving a few more streets out of town it's like living in the Dark Ages.

There's a knock on the door, and I look at what time it is. I figured everyone would be asleep by now since it's pretty late.

"How are you settling in?" Torrance asks when I open the door. "Sorry Bonnie tricked you into staying. I know you were planning on staying at the BnB."

"It's fine. I would feel better if I could call them and tell them I won't be coming, though."

Torrance waves me off. "Oh, don't worry about that. They'll know where you are."

I quirk my eyebrow. I seem to do that a lot when I am with Torrance.

"Ms. Luella's daughter and son-in-law own the BnB, and Jasper helps out when needed."

"Of course they do," I bark out a laugh. "This is small town life."

"No. This is teeny tiny town life. It's different. Small towns have at least some privacies. Valley Creek does not. Everyone knows everyone. And pretty much everyone has lived here their entire life or knew someone who did before moving here. And—" She stops mid-thought. "Why are you looking at me like that?"

"Like what?"

"Like you've never talked to me before."

Had I been looking at her a certain way? I didn't think I had, but then again I have been wondering a lot lately about how much I really know about Torrance. We might have met nine years ago, but we've hardly spent any time together and even less of that was willingly.

"We haven't. Not really."

"I guess you're right. Okay, rapid-fire questions. You get five."

"Five questions?"

"Mmhmm."

"And you'll answer anything I ask?"

"Within reason. And only if I get to ask you five in return."

I put my hand out and surprisingly she takes it, so we shake on it. And I try not to dwell on how soft her hand is in mine or how well it fits.

"How many languages do you speak?"

"Fluently? Five, but I can get by with…let's go with nine?"

"I'm going to need more details for this to work."

Torrence huffs, but she comes more fully into my room and sits on the edge of the bed. "Fine, but I'm not standing the whole time if you're going to make me give a thesis on each answer."

I sit in the chair opposite and gesture for her to continue.

"My father is from Mexico and speaks Spanish, my mother's family is obviously French, and I grew up with English as their common language. Then in high school I decided to take German as my foreign language credits. When we got to college, we decided American Sign Language would be the perfect class to take as roommates. Then I went through a brief hockey stage, so I took up Russian."

I'm sure my eyes are bugged out. "Wow."

Torrance shrugs. "Once upon a time I contemplated going into linguistics."

"What changed your mind?"

"Is this another question or am I still giving a thesis?"

"You choose."

"Fine. I decided that unless I ended up working for the FBI or CIA, being a linguist wasn't exactly a fruitful job. And frankly, I'd hate living out of a suitcase and not being able to call my friends or sister. Just because I like spy movies doesn't mean I'd be a good spy."

I laugh. I can't help it. I've done that a few times since we've been in Valley Creek. It's kind of a strange sensation. I don't think I've freely laughed this much in a very long time. Maybe everyone was right. I do need a break from work and studying. Though I should be studying now and not sitting here with Torrance. Not that I want her to stop talking. Strangely, I don't.

"The thought of me as a spy that amusing?"

I shake my head.

"Then what's so funny?"

"I think it's funny that we can have a conversation like this and not argue once. We can even have multiple text conversations and keep the peace. So why—"

"So why can't we get along when we are in the car? Or in life in general?"

"Exactly! Why did we keep arguing today?"

"Well, you were hangry."

"I believe it all started with you being miffed at the radio for not being exactly what you wanted, like a playlist would be."

Torrance stands and squares her shoulders like she's ready for a fight. It's only now that I realize I'm mirroring her posture. When did I even stand up? Is arguing with her that instinctual that I don't even realize when I'm doing it anymore?

I huff out a breath. "There's no need for us to get agitated all over again over what has already happened. How about we just agree to let the past be in the past and move forward?"

"Agreed. I should let you get some sleep. I know it's late." Torrance turns to leave then pauses, turning back glancing over towards where my suitcase is sitting. "What was in the bag that Millie gave you?"

"No idea. I haven't looked in it yet. She just told me it would help me get through traveling with you. Seems you have quite the reputation of being a difficult traveler."

Torrance rolls her eyes. "That's because when Millie travels, she likes to get up before the sun so she can soak up all the day has to offer or whatever Disney princess crap she likes to spin. I, on the other hand, would rather sleep in and take my time. I'll still get where I'm going, but I'd rather it be on my terms rather than anyone else's."

"So, what you're saying is no early mornings, and as long as we do whatever you want to do, you'll be pleasant?"

"Exactly! See there's hope for you yet, Porter."

I snort a laugh. "You're something else."

Torrance mock bows. "Thank you for noticing. Now I really will let you go, because as much as I hate being woken up, I have a firecracker of a niece who will storm into my room in approximately six hours, and she will be raring to go."

A BINDER. A freaking binder! My curiosity finally got the better of me, and I had to know what was in that bag Millie had given me. It's a full on "Survival Guide" with colored tabs and everything. Torrance is a full-grown woman, and her best friend and roommate not only gave me a survival guide but had one at the ready? Who does that?

I don't even have the mental fortitude to dig into all of it. I barely glance over the table of contents, because there is one, and close the three-inch, fluorescent orange blinder. It's so bright that if I'm not careful, I'll inadvertently guide a plane to land. Okay, so that's a little dramatic, but it is an eye sore. I shove it back into the bag.

It's been a long day with all the travel and then the unexpected turn of events that led me to staying at Torrance's grandmother's house rather than the BnB that I was planning on. I will admit that this evening has been much better than I expected. And that conversation tonight was, well, rather confusing actually. It's like that day at my apartment. Like we were almost flirting, but it's Torrance, and we don't do that. Tonight was the woman I've been texting and not the woman I was in the car with today. It's starting to feel like there are two different people, and I'm not sure what that means for the rest of this road trip. I'm equal parts intrigued and scared to find out.

CHAPTER 16

Torrance

"**I**T'S MY BIRTHDAY!!!!" Aly screams down the hallway bright and early Saturday morning. I'm awake just enough to not be completely taken by surprise when she busts down my door and pounces on my bed, jumping up and down.

She continues jumping as she starts singing her own version of the birthday song. I'm way too tired to function, but I can't help but smile as she joyously hops up and down.

Aly finishes her song and lands with a harumph. "Oreo, guess what?!"

"Chicken butt!"

"Oreo," Aly giggles, "you're silly!"

"I'm not silly." I start wiggling my fingers as I start to move towards her. "But I am the tickle monster!"

Aly shrieks and giggles, and I tickle her until she can't catch her breath.

"Oreo, you didn't give a real guess," she laughs as she lays on my bed next to me.

"I'm sorry. What was it you wanted me to guess about?"

"Jasper is coming over, and he's going to take me to go horseback riding. On a real horse!"

"A real horse! That's pretty nice of Jasper."

Aly nods her head emphatically. "Uh huh. He asked Mommy last night if it was okay. I wasn't supposed to know about it, so I have to act surprised when he comes over to ask me if I want to go."

I try to hide my smile.

"I'll try to keep your secret," I tell my niece, knowing full well that there isn't a person alive in a twelve-mile radius that wouldn't have heard her screaming this morning. If my sister didn't realize that Aly knows about the "surprise," she does now.

"Thanks," Aly says with all the seriousness of a grown adult. "I wouldn't want to hurt Jasper's feelings. He's my best friend."

"Hey, I thought I was your best friend?" I protest in mock offense.

"You're my Oreo." She hops on my lap and gives me the tightest hug. "And my most favoritest aunt ever!"

She gives my cheek a big kiss. Gosh, I love this kid so dang much. I squeeze her back. I have a lot of feelings about my sister's ex, none of them pleasant, but there is one thing I can't deny. Without that loser of a human being, Carson wouldn't have Aly, and all of our lives would be far less without her.

"I guess I can work with that." I give her another squeeze.

Aly looks at me with all seriousness again. "Is Potato your boyfriend?"

"Who?"

"Potato? Mommy said you'd be blind not to see how handsome he is."

"You mean Porter?" I'm going to kill my sister for talking.

"Yeah. She and Bonnie were talking last night in the kitchen when they were cleaning the dishes."

"Oh, were they? And what else were Mommy and Bonnie talking about?" I'm suddenly very grateful for my niece's overly attentive nature.

Aly shrugs. "Something about you turning into a splinter and that if you aren't careful a good man is going to go to waste right under your nose."

Oh, that's it. My sister is going to get it now. I wonder if I can still video chat Aly if I'm in prison? I shift my weight and get out of the bed. No need for coffee this morning. I'm full of enough indignation and rage, no caffeine required.

Aly hops out of the bed and is right on my heels. When the two of us make our way into the dining room, we have completely opposite expressions.

I hear a faint, "Wow!" in the back of my mind, but all I'm seeing is red. My sister must sense that my rage is towards her because one look at me and she puts her hands up in defense.

"I know you're mad, and you have every right to be, but it's Aly's day. You wouldn't want to make her an orphan on her birthday."

When she says it, it sounds melodramatic and over the top, but it does the trick, and I simmer down. I hate how much Carson knows me. Not really. I actually love it, but I'm mad at her, so I hate it.

"We aren't done talking about this."

"Completely fair."

As I start to think more clearly, I realize that there is no way Carson knows why I was so mad, which means she was apologizing for something she thought I would be mad about. Which tells me that there is a whole lot more going on than I thought. I don't have time to confront her before Jasper walks through the door carrying a bouquet of wildflowers and an entire bushel of apples. Aly immediately drops the pastry she was trying to sneak from the platter Bonnie placed on the table and runs towards him.

"Are those for me?" Aly's eyes are the size of saucers as she stares at Jasper in wonderment.

"That depends." He gives her an inquisitive look. "These are special birthday flowers. I can only give them to special birthday girls who are turning four. Do you know anyone who fits that description?"

"Me!" Aly squeals. "It's my birthday! And I'm four!"

"You are? Well, isn't that lucky. I thought I was going to have to ride my horse all the way over to Dunway to find someone to give these to."

Okay, fine. He can be her best friend. But I'll fight to the death to stay Oreo.

"What's with the apples?" I jump as Porter's breath tickles the back of my neck. I hadn't even heard him come into the room, never mind him standing close enough to whisper into my ear.

"Sorry," he whispers again. "Didn't mean to scare you."

And yet he didn't move any further away. He's still standing right next to me. Out of the corner of my eye, I see Bonnie watching us and nudging Carson.

I take a much-needed step away from Porter. I rub my arms trying to get rid of the goose bumps. I don't even dare look Porter in the eye. I don't know what has been going on the last twelve hours, but it needs to stop. I'm not and will never be interested in him. I might not go out often, but I know a player when I see one. Porter is always surrounded by women hanging all over him, and he has been since college. I've seen and experienced firsthand the heartbreak that comes from falling for an overt flirt. When I fall in love, it will be with a man who only has eyes for me and won't try to take care of or fix me. I'm not looking for a second half; I'm looking for a complimentary piece. Like a puzzle.

I clear my throat. "Looks like we have a birthday breakfast to get to." I look down at Aly. "That is, if you're still interested in celebrating your big day?"

"Yes!" Aly screams, just like I knew she would, bringing all of the attention back to her and off of me. Aly runs up to Jasper and grabs his hand. "Come this way and sit with me!"

Jasper smiles down at her lovingly and follows without question.

Aly stops briefly and turns to face the rest of us, urging, "Come on!"

We all laugh and follow after her. Everyone starts to fill into the seats around the table.

"Sit next to me, Potato."

Porter looks at me, confused. "Am I Potato?"

Aly rolls her eyes like it's obvious. "Duh."

I don't even try to hide my amusement at his reaction to his nickname.

"You should feel honored," Carson says laughing. "Aly only gives nicknames to people she really likes. You've made quite the impression if she's already giving you one."

"I'll wear it with honor." He bows at the birthday girl, and a little bit of my heart squeezes at the sight.

Carson wraps her arms around my waist. "Are you sure you don't like him? Because, girl, that man is something else."

I roll my eyes and wriggle out of her arms. "I'm sure. Now why don't we focus on your daughter since it's her day?"

Carson swats at my butt. "Fine, but this isn't over."

I would be surprised if it was.

CHAPTER 17

Porter

"THANKS FOR INVITING me along." I look over at Jasper as we dismount our horses and Aly takes off to collect wildflowers. I wasn't expecting an invite to join him and Aly on her birthday ride, but it was nice to get out of the house. And honestly, it was nice to get away from Torrance.

As confused as I have been about her over the last few interactions we have had, the last 24 hours have been high on the list. What was with me this morning? Why did I choose to stand so close to her and whisper in her ear? It was a very flirty and intimate thing to do. I don't know what came over me. And I know I'm not the only one who was affected by it. I heard the shuddered breath. And I noticed that she didn't step away from me right away. When she did, I feel like it had more to do with her grandmother and sister watching us than anything else.

"No problem. Aly was more than excited to invite you along when I mentioned it." He gives me a pointed look. "And it looked like you could use a break from the Rodriquez sisters."

I huff out a laugh. "They're something else."

Jasper laughs. "That they are. I've only seen Torrance a few times over the years, but Carson and Aly talk about her all the time."

"So, you and Carson?" I ask. I don't want to pry, but it's obvious that something is going on. At least that there is a want for something on his end.

"Are just friends," Jasper says as if on autopilot.

"Ah." I can tell there's more, but I'm not going to press. I just met the man yesterday, and it's clear he values his privacy which I can respect.

"Don't get me wrong," Jaspers continues. "Carson is amazing, but her sole focus is on Aly. As it should be. Someday she'll be ready to date again, and then, well, I'm not sure what I'll do."

I nod with understanding. "They're lucky to have you."

Jasper looks over to where Aly is collecting her flowers. "She's a pretty great kid."

"She seems it. How long have you been in Valley Creek?" I ask, sensing Jasper's need for a change in subject.

"About five years now." He gives me a wry smile. "I came to visit a friend who grew up here, and I liked it so much I decided to stay."

"Small towns are like that."

"You sound like you know from experience."

"Grew up in a small town outside of Memphis. My grandparents own a farm out there."

"Well, that explains where you learned to ride a horse."

I laugh. "My mother was adamant that I wouldn't get within ten feet of a horse, and I didn't, until I was about ten."

"What happened when you were ten?"

My brain shudders at the memory.

Dad had taken off for good this time. Mom started feeling sick again and went to the doctor. It was cancer and spreading quickly. My sister was only two. I was mad and sure that somehow Mom getting sick was my father's fault. I knew logically it couldn't be, but I didn't want to think logically. I just wanted to be a kid and not have to be responsible for things my friends didn't have to worry about.

Grandpa Gentry came into my room one morning and told me to get dressed. I had popped off with some sort of attitude, and he just leveled me with a stare.

"Sorry," I muttered.

"You're hurtin', and you're mad. Just don't make it a habit. Now get dressed and meet me downstairs."

When I came downstairs, he wasn't there. I walked through the whole house looking for him. When I came into the kitchen, I found Mom and MarMar sitting at the table. They smiled when they saw me.

"Good morning, sweetheart." Mom stood and hugged me, kissing my temple.

"Your grandfather is out in the barn," MarMar said as if she knew what I was going to ask. She probably did. There was very little that she and Grandpa Gentry didn't talk about. "He's waiting for you by the horses."

I looked over at my mom. When we moved in with my grandparents she had one rule: no horses. She had had a friend get injured when they were kids, and she wouldn't go near them. And neither had I.

She nodded. "Go ahead, Porter. It's okay."

That's the day that my grandfather insisted on teaching me that there was more to life than just me and my life.

"If it's personal then you don't have to answer. I don't mean to pry."

I look back at Jasper. "I was an angry kid. My grandfather decided that the best way to teach me to look outside of myself was to help take care of the horses like his dad had done with him."

Jasper nods.

We don't talk much the rest of our time out on the ride. It isn't awkward, quite the opposite. It is kind of nice to have that level of understanding with someone. I don't have many people in my life who could sit in silence. Duncan and Trent certainly can't.

From time-to-time, Aly makes comments about what she sees or whatever thoughts pop into her head. We're almost back to the house when I have a nagging question for the little tike.

"Hey, Aly?"

"What, Potato?"

I smile. "Why do you call me Potato? I get that it's a nickname, but nicknames come from somewhere. Like I assume there's a reason why you call your aunt Oreo."

"Oh, that's easy. I call her Oreo because she calls me Kitty Kat, and cats like milk."

I still don't understand, but thankfully Jasper can interpret.

"According to the Oreo cookie slogan, milk's favorite cookie is Oreo," he explains.

"Ah, I see." I still don't, but I have never claimed to understand the logic of females or children, so a female child is obviously going to confuse the heck out of me.

"So why do you call me Potato?" I ask again, though I'm not sure I'll understand even if she explains it.

"Because two weeks ago Mommy and Oreo were talking on the phone, and they were talking about how you were going on a trip, and then Oreo said something about some guy named Mr. Collins and boiled potatoes." I think she's done, but then she takes a big breath and continues on. One thing is for certain, this family is full of women who know how to talk. "And then when you got here yesterday, Mommy and Bonnie were talking and said you were one hot potato."

I wait for more of an explanation, but apparently that's it. Much to my chagrin I know exactly what potato quote she is referring to, because Torrance was quoting my sister's favorite movie. And honestly, I expected better from Torrance. The fact that I am technically a Mr. Collins is low hanging fruit. But I do find it interesting that one look at me, and Carson and their grandmother were on my side. It makes me wonder what all Torrance has said about me. Amara wasn't wrong when she said Torrance was a puzzle I can't figure out.

AFTER GETTING BACK from our ride, the whole house had been transformed into a kid's paradise. If I thought Aly was loud before, it doesn't hold a candle to the shrieks of joy. It would be overwhelming if she hadn't grown on me so quickly.

I stay back for most of the party, partly because people, especially strangers, aren't really my thing, and partly because I like seeing Torrance in her element. I've seen her with her friends and roommates, but it's completely different seeing her with her family.

With her roommates, she's such a strong personality who doesn't take no for an answer, at least not without a fight. With her family, she's compassionate and listens. Sure, her and her sister argue, mostly in Spanish and French, but they still move forward even when they don't agree. I'm sure she is all those things with her friends as well, but I haven't seen it much.

I'm starting to think I've made my judgements on false or incomplete perceptions. It's like when we have a patient with a complicated case. There is more than meets the eye and more than is skin deep. We have to dig a little deeper to understand what it is. And that's just what I plan on doing on this road trip.

We've got nothing but time ahead of us.

CHAPTER 18

Torrance

I WAKE UP TO my sister kneeing me in the back. She insisted on sleeping in here hours after Aly fell asleep during our girls' night. Bonnie went to sleep shortly after dinner; the hords of children all afternoon really took it out of her. Aly made it through the nail painting, but we lost her during the movie. I'm pretty sure Carson picked the movie just for that purpose.

I look at my fresh manicure as I stretch my arms over my head then turn to shove Carson back to her side of the bed.

She wakes with a groan. "Watch it!"

"You're on my side."

She slowly opens one eye to peer over at me. "Sorry. I'm not used to sharing a bed."

"And I am?" I deadpan.

Carson sits up with a smirk. "I know of someone who wouldn't mind sharing a bed with you."

I roll my eyes. Two can play this game.

"I think you're confused because you know who wouldn't mind sharing a bed with *you*? I'll give you one guess. He's about 6'1", built like a house. Always around. Looks at your daughter like she's his."

Carson is fully sitting up now.

"So how long of a drive do you have today?"

"You can't just change the topic."

"I can, and I will."

I sit up so we are shoulder to shoulder, bumping into her. "You started it."

"And now I'm finishing it."

There's no point in arguing, not when I need to get up and ready to head out. I hate that I have so little time with her on this trip, but I am grateful for the extra time we gained by Porter coming along.

The last couple of days with my family have been just what I needed. An unexpected but pleasant surprise of the trip is Porter. The way he's been with my grandmother, how he's taken the time to talk to her and the fact that he willingly sat through her French lessons when she learned that he tried (and failed) to learn back in college... I didn't see any of that coming.

Don't even get me started on how he's been with Aly. She just about adores him. Even Carson is taken by him. If she wasn't so smitten with Jasper, like I know she is, I think she'd be some major competition... not that there is any need for that... or... what is happening?

Two days of us getting along and borderline flirting, and I'm suddenly twitter-pated? Nope. Not happening. I've known Porter for nine years. It's going to take much more than him winning over my family for me to do a full 180 on my opinions.

I jump out of bed. There is no reason why my thoughts should be going there. It's because of Carson's stupid comment. That's all it is.

I grab my stuff and head towards the bathroom to get ready. The sooner we get on the road the sooner we get to our destination and our very separate rooms.

"ONE LAST HUG," Bonnie says through tears after breakfast. She really out-did herself this morning. She puts any commercial bakery to shame.

Bonnie is always emotional when I have to leave. Not that I'm not, I just don't show it as freely as she does. I wish I could; I don't know why I can't seem to show how I'm feeling. Probably has something to do with the fact that I never was really able to as a kid. Mom and Dad are great at a lot of things but giving emotional support wasn't one of them.

Bonnie lets me go, kissing my cheeks. "Ma chère fille."

"Au revoir, Grand-mère. Je t'aime."

"Porter, venez ici," she waves her hand beckoning him closer. "It was so kind of you to come. Come back any time."

"Thank you for such a warm welcome."

Bonnie pats his cheek, and he leans down for her to kiss it. Before he straightens, she whispers something in his ear. I can't hear what she says, but the tips of his ears go pink.

"Drive safely and take your time," she says to both of us. "You never know what will happen on a long journey."

Then she winks. A nice, sweet moment, and she had to

ruin it with a wink. Oh, that woman! I love her dearly, but man, is she something else.

Porter finishes loading up the SUV with our bags while I go give Carson and Aly final hugs.

"Do you really need to go, Oreo?"

"I'm afraid so, Kitty Kat, but I'll be back to visit soon. And we will FaceTime and message like we usually do."

She gives me the biggest hug she can muster.

"What about Potato?"

"What about him?"

"Will he be coming back with you?"

"Oh, I don't think so. This was just a one-time thing, Aly."

She lets go of me just enough to look up at me with her big brown eyes. "It doesn't have to be. He's nice, Oreo. You could like him."

If only she understood just how dangerous of a suggestion that is.

"You're right. She could," my sister interrupts. She gives me a pointed look. "He's a good guy, Tor. Give him a chance."

I shake my head. "We've been through this. I won't get involved with someone who isn't ready for commitment."

"And I'll say what I've said every other time: who's to say he isn't?"

"The hundreds of dates he goes on is a good start."

She waves off my comment. "First, have you actually seen him on all these dates, or is it conjecture? And second, even if it is true, all that proves is that he hasn't found anyone he wants to spend more time with. Doesn't mean he doesn't want someone to commit to, just that he hasn't found that right person."

"Or he doesn't want to," I say incredulously.

"*Or* he *has* found her, and she won't give him a chance because of something he said one time as a stupid college freshman."

"It wasn't just one time," I argue.

"Then give him some grace, Tori. He's not a kid, anymore than you are. We grow up. We learn from our mistakes; we've lived our lives. It only does so much if the people around us don't let us forget about past mistakes."

"I can't just forget the past, Carson."

"Okay, fine. But that doesn't mean the past has to dictate the future. The man standing over there," she points towards Porter who is talking with Jasper, "isn't the same guy you've talked about over the years."

"I guess."

After one last big hug for my sister, I head to the car.

I grab Jasper's hand. "Keep an eye on them?"

"Of course."

I look over at Carson as she bends down to talk to Aly. "Give her time, Jasper. She'll come around."

He smiles at me. "I'll give her time, if you give him a chance."

I look over at Porter.

Jasper continues, "You and I are a lot alike. It's hard to trust people after being hurt and seeing people we care about hurt in the past." He squeezes my hand. "I don't mean to overstep. I just thought I should say something."

"You didn't overstep. You're right, it is hard." I dare myself to look him in the face. "I'm not making any promises, but I'll think about it."

"Sometimes that's all it takes."

"You ready to head out?" Porter asks.

"Yeah. We've got a long day of driving ahead." I smile one more time at Jasper before I climb into the passenger seat.

Porter gets in and starts the car. "Ready?"

I nod. And we pull out onto the road.

WE DRIVE IN silence through town. It doesn't feel awkward exactly, but it's also not totally comfortable. We haven't spent time alone since the other night in his room and that was...what was that? Porter is different this trip than I thought he would be. I don't mind him being in my space. My family clearly loves him, which is also a problem because they haven't stopped bringing up all of his "fine qualities," as Bonnie kept putting it last night.

I just need to get my family's gushing words of approval out of my head. Which will be easier once we are out of Valley Creek. And you know, once my sister stops texting me about it.

> **CARSON:** Talk to him already.

> **TORRANCE:** How do you know we aren't talking?

> **CARSON:** Are you?

TORRANCE: No, but there is no way of you knowing that unless you bugged the car.

TORRANCE: You didn't bug the car, did you?

CARSON: Of course not.

CARSON: I have people for that.

TORRANCE: Tell Jasper he's fired.

CARSON: I just know you. You think something or someone is one way, and when you learn something new, it takes you a bit to adjust.

TORRANCE: I do not.

CARSON: So you haven't seen a new side of Porter the last couple of days?

TORRANCE: Will you get out of my head?

CARSON: Not until you admit that you were wrong about him.

TORRANCE: I'll admit to that when you admit that you're more than friends with Jasper.

CARSON: You're the worst.

> **TORRANCE:** Right back at ya.

> **CARSON:** Call me when you stop for the night.

> **TORRANCE:** Will do. Love you.

> **CARSON:** Love you too.

> **CARSON:** Just give him a chance. I mean, you're stuck in a car for the next three days. Might as well make good use of the time.

> **CARSON:** And maybe make out for a few hours...

I cough as I read Carson's last text, making me spray water all over myself. I sit up more fully as I try to find some napkins. This car is immaculate, which I'm sure is Porter's doing and not Trent's. I haven't seen him much since high school, but I just don't see him becoming some neat freak. Porter, on the other hand...

"Here." Porter reaches across the now-open center console with a stack of napkins.

"Thanks." Thankfully, my legs took the brunt of the water, so it doesn't take much to clean everything up. Now if only my face would calm down and stop burning. I don't blush easily, but with how hot my face is feeling, I have to be as red as a lobster.

"You okay?" Porter's deep voice makes me jump. Not because I forgot he was sitting next to me—the complete opposite in fact. I'm more embarrassed knowing he saw me spit all over myself than actually spraying water.

"Mmhmm."

I really wish Carson would just get out of my head. I'm confused enough about Porter without adding in all of her thoughts on the subject. Not to mention that last text. I pull out my phone and delete it. Last thing I need is Porter somehow seeing it.

Sometimes I wish I didn't tell my sister everything. We didn't used to share so much; I've always loved my sister, but when you're four years apart, there are things you just don't talk about with your younger sister. We've definitely gotten closer the older we've gotten, especially since Aly was born.

"Did you have a nice time with your sister last night?

"We did. See?" I wiggle my fingers in front of his face. He bats them out of the way then promptly puts both hands back on the wheel. I huff out a laugh because of course Porter drives with his hands at ten and two.

"They're orange."

"My favorite color."

"No one's favorite color is orange." Porter glances towards me.

"I guess I'm no one because mine is." I motion towards my water bottle, purse, phone case, and blanket I have shoved down at my feet.

Porter smirks. "I stand corrected."

"What did you do last night?"

"Figured I should get some studying in before things got too crazy this week."

I hear a voice that suspiciously sounds like Carson in my head telling me to keep the conversation going and get to know him a little better.

"You said before we left that you were going to study. What are you studying for? Aren't you done with school?"

Porter looks over at me again. "Do you really want to know?"

"Yes, I really want to know."

He gives me a look.

"What? We agreed to get along, remember? This is me trying to get along with you."

Porter gives a half smirk as he turns his attention back to the road. And there is a part of me that gets butterflies at the sight.

"I'm working towards becoming a PA."

"PA? Political advocate?"

"Physician assistant," Porter corrects me, but not with the usual tone he usually gives me when he corrects me.

I fight back a smile.

Porter looks over at me. "You were messing with me, weren't you?"

I let my laugh loose. "I'm sorry. It was way too easy!"

He gives me a full grin this time, and oh my, there is a full flock of butterflies. Do butterflies fly in flocks, or is that just birds? Whatever it is, a whole bunch of butterflies are flying around my insides just at the sight of his smile, and I need them to calm down. Nothing has changed. He might not be as terrible as I thought he was, but it's not like I'm going to jump right in with wanting to date him. He's still a ladies' man, and I don't want that.

Porter's phone lights up with two notifications, one reading Sloane and the other reading Zion, as if to prove my point. Porter ignores them.

"You can check your phone if you need to," I say, though part of me really doesn't want to. Just to prove that it doesn't matter to me, I add, "Or I can read it to you since you're driving."

He shakes his head.

"I don't mean to be nosy, just trying to be helpful." I sound defensive, and I hate it. I really was just trying to be helpful. Even if part of me wants to claw out the eyes of whoever these girls are. Not that I'm jealous, because there is no need to be jealous. They can have him. I don't want him. Those butterflies can take flight right on out of here.

"It's fine. It's not important."

Another message from Sloane chimes in.

"Are you sure?"

Porter silences his phone. "Positive."

I really try not to dwell on who Sloane and Zion are, but it's as if I'm obsessed with knowing. But I'm not about to ask. Are they girls he's dated? More than dated? Were they at the club when I saw him that one time? I am full on spiraling when Porter breaks through my tumbling thoughts.

"So what do we have to do to get you to put on this playlist you've been planning?"

Music. The perfect distraction.

"Where's the cord for me to plug it in?"

"Here," Porter passes me the cord blindly, his hand brushing mine. I will not, and I mean *not*, be thinking about what that slight contact does to my insides.

"What's on today's playlist?" Porter asks. "You said you made one for each day?"

"I did. Nothing is worse than listening to the same thing over and over again while on a road trip."

I hit play and let the music fill the car. I refrain from singing too much, but I hum along and sing some of the words to myself as we drive. Porter and I don't really talk, letting the scenery pass us by as we drive. Any easiness we had disappeared as soon as those messages came in. It's not like it's just me; Porter hasn't said anything either.

"I'm thinking we stop in a bit to get something to eat and top off the gas tank. What do you think?" Porter asks. He sounds a little timid, but I guess after the last time we had a similar conversation I can understand why he would be. I really was a brat that first day.

"That sounds good. It will feel good to get out and stretch for a bit."

We're basically in the middle of nowhere, and there aren't too many options, but Porter sees a sign for a gas station and a nearby diner and exits. As soon as he parks the car, I make the excuse that I need to pee and bolt for the bathroom. I don't, at least not that badly, but he doesn't need to know that. I need to clear my head and more than anything I need some space from him.

CHAPTER 19

Porter

N O SOONER HAD I parked the car to get gas than Torrance raced out of the vehicle. I don't know what's going on. We were in a good rhythm, we were talking, even joking and laughing, and then Sloane started blowing up my phone and Torrance got weird. I don't understand. I also don't want to ask and risk her going back to what her usual response is to me. We've had a good weekend. Great, in fact. I definitely didn't expect to like her family as much as I did. And thanks to Torrance and Carson not knowing I understood what they were saying, I was able to hear some of what they were talking about. I know it's kind of a jerk move to eavesdrop, but is it really eavesdropping if they are talking right in front of you? I mean, I know technically they were talking in a different language that they assume I don't speak, but I can't be held responsible for their assumptions.

My phone dings again with another notification from my sister.

ZION: Are you sure you can't stop by on your way through?

ZION: I have my music showcase tonight, and it would mean a lot if you could be there.

ZION: Are you ignoring me?

ZION: You'd tell me if you were ignoring me, wouldn't you?

ZION: I guess you wouldn't, but still. It's rather rude to ignore your ONLY sister like this.

ZION: Come on, Porter, please come. It would mean a lot. You haven't been to any of my shows since high school. You're already driving through town. What's a two-hour delay in an already long drive?

ZION: I'm not above begging

PORTER: Will you chill? I was driving. Driving and texting is illegal for a reason.

ZION: So you'll come to my showcase?!

PORTER: I don't know, Zi, I have a long drive ahead of me. And it's not just up to me.

ZION: Oh, right, MarMar said you were traveling with your girlfriend.

PORTER: Torrance isn't my girlfriend.

ZION: But you want her to be.

PORTER: Why does everyone keep saying that?

ZION: Because it's true, even if you won't admit it.

PORTER: There's nothing to admit.

ZION: Face it, big bro, we know you better than you know yourself.

I roll my eyes. Little sisters. We're eight years apart and have very little in common, but I'd still do anything for her. I'll ask Torrance about stopping by to see her, but I'm not sure about staying for her showcase. That would just put us so far behind schedule in our drive.

PORTER: I'll talk to Torrance about stopping by to see you, but I'm not making any promises about the showcase.

ZION: YAY!!!

I finish filling up the gas tank and move the car right as Torrance heads back out of the gas station. I point towards the diner that is next door, and she nods.

Torrance and I sit in silence as the waitress hands us our menus and takes our order. Things have been awkward since my phone started blowing up with messages. It's as if we were in a bubble, and those dings were the pins that popped it.

Speaking of, my phone dings with another notification. I swear I'm never this popular on a normal day so why can't this stupid rectangle stay quiet today?

I sigh as I read Sloane's name. What on earth does she want? I have multiple messages from her. I haven't read them yet, but anything more than two is excessive considering I only hang out with her when Trent is around. And we never talk outside of that. The only reason she has my number is because she planned a massive surprise birthday party for Trent last year and needed my help to get him to the party.

I read through the messages.

> **SLOANE:** How's the road trip going?

> **SLOANE:** Are you and Tori getting along?

> **SLOANE:** You aren't answering so that means you're either driving or it's going REALLY well.

A gif of some cartoon character I don't recognize lifts his eyebrows suggestively.

I realize that I don't know Sloane super well, but I think I know her well enough to find these texts out of character and rather crass. Before I can reply, another text comes in.

> **SLOANE:** Porter! I'm so sorry! Trent forgot his phone charger at the gym and took over mine.

> **SLOANE:** OMG!!! I just saw the gif!!!! I'm so embarrassed!!

Well, that makes much more sense. These are exactly the type of text messages I would expect to get from my cousin.

> **PORTER:** The only person who should be sorry and embarrassed is my idiot cousin.

> **SLOANE:** He is!

> **PORTER:** I highly doubt that.

> **SLOANE:** Since I have you here, how are things going?

> **PORTER:** Unless either of you have anything of actual importance to tell me, please stop blowing up my phone. It's distracting and frankly annoying.

> **SLOANE:** Sloane here. We are very sorry for bothering you and promise not to message you unless it is anything vital.

I could respond, but that seems like it would only encourage them further, so I put my phone back down on the table. I look up to see Torrance watching me. She doesn't say anything, but that cool scrutinizing look that I have known for so many years is back. After seeing what she is like when she has her guard down, it makes this feel even more unsettling. I know I don't owe her an explanation, it's not like I know everything she's been doing on her phone since we've been driving today, but I still feel the need to explain.

"Sorry about that," I say.

Torrance shrugs. "It's no bother to me."

Lies. It clearly bothers her. I just don't know why. I know why I hope it bothers her, but it's ridiculous to think things could change so drastically in three days.

"That was Sloane."

"I don't care who you text, Porter," she says, annoyed.

I swear I see her jaw tick as she says the words. Clearly the idea of Sloane texting me bothers her. Then it occurs to me that she has no idea who Sloane is. As far as she knows it's some woman I'm seeing or at least spending time with. Which would only bother her if she was jealous. Could she be jealous of the idea of me dating someone? Only one way to find out, but I'm not going to just flat out and ask her. That would be way too embarrassing if I was wrong.

"Sloane is dating my cousin," I say as casually as I can.

Torrance's face relaxes then scrunches in confusion. "If she's dating your cousin then why is she texting you?"

I try to hold in my amusement. She is jealous. At least a little. "Trent got ahold of her phone. Some excuse of losing or forgetting his charger. I think he knew I wouldn't answer his messages, and since Sloane isn't insane, he probably figured I would answer hers."

Torrance rolls her eyes. "Some things never change. Trent never thought through things fully in high school."

"Does anyone? I mean, how many high school students do you know who not only know exactly what they want in life but also have the maturity to go out and make it happen?"

"I don't know. I don't think I was an immature teenager. Not that I knew exactly what I wanted in life, but I certainly knew what I didn't want."

"I can see that."

"See what?"

"That you were a stubborn teenager who thought she knew what she was doing," I tease.

Torrance rolls her eyes again, but I see a slight smirk at the corner of her mouth.

Torrance reaches out her hand across the table towards me.

"Hi, Pot. I'm Kettle," she says dryly.

I can't contain the laugh that erupts from me as I take her hand. I will myself not to focus on how nice her hand feels in mine when I notice several pairs of eyes turning to look at me, but none of that matters once I see the smile that stretches across Torrance's face. I don't think I've ever seen her smile. Not fully. And certainly not directed towards me. It's a sight to behold. Her whole face lights up, and her green eyes shine. I don't think I ever realized that her eyes were green. I always thought they were more of a stormy hazel, but they are green.

I take a few steading breaths before I'm able to stop laughing. I haven't laughed that hard and that long in a long time. "I guess we aren't as opposite as we thought."

"I guess not." We sit in silence just looking at each other when our waitress comes back over with drinks. "Can I ask a random question?"

"How random are we talking?" I ask.

"Something that I probably should know by now, but since we haven't exactly been friends all these years, I don't."

"Well, my interest is peaked."

"Why are you and Duncan friends?"

I choke on my water as I take a drink. I'm not sure what I was expecting, but that wasn't it. I catch my breath and look up at her. She's a blank canvas. No readable emotions on her face. She just sits there and waits for me to answer.

"Um, I guess the simple answer is that his grandparents are friends with my grandparents, and when they learned that we would be going to the same college, they decided we needed to meet. We became roommates, and I guess that was that."

Torrance nods. "That makes sense. I wouldn't have become friends with Amara and Kiersten if we hadn't been roommates."

"Having roommates, especially ones that are so different from you, can be a challenge, but it wasn't all bad. I definitely would have been more of a hermit if it wouldn't have been for him."

"You, a hermit?" Torrance asks with disbelief.

She really doesn't know me, does she? I guess I can't be surprised. I'm not exactly easy to get to know.

"I'm not exactly a people person. Add in that I'd rather stay home than go out, the fact that he got me out of our apartment as much as he did is a miracle."

I see the wheels turning in her head. Before I can say anything else, our waitress comes back with our food. Torrance takes a few bites of her french fries before she speaks.

"How much further do we have to go today?"

"I was actually going to talk to you about that. My sister is going to school a couple hours away and was wondering if we could stop by on our way through. I told her I wasn't sure, but I would ask you."

"Yeah. Why wouldn't we go see your sister?"

"I mean, it would put us behind schedule. We would have to drive when it's dark, which I know is something we were trying to avoid."

"Well, if we're going to be that close to your sister, then I think you should go see her."

"Are you sure?"

"Porter, we just spent multiple days with my family. I think we've established how important I think family is. Tell your sister we will come through town."

I send a quick message to Zion telling her we would come by. If all caps and multiple dancing gifs are any indication, I'd say she's a little excited.

CHAPTER 20

Torrance

WHEN PORTER MENTIONED going to see his sister, I didn't think twice about saying yes, but maybe I should have. This town looks all but abandoned. I'm talking ghost town levels of activity. I think we saw more people at the truck stop a couple hours back than I've seen since we got off the highway.

"Is this where you reveal you're actually a serial killer?" I'm mostly joking, but the thought had crossed my mind.

"Yes," Porter deadpans. "I drove all this way to off you. I wanted to ensure I was the only suspect in the case."

I feel the corner of my mouth twitch. Who knew the man had such a dark sense of humor? I'm about to ask where we're going when I hear a high-pitched squeal running towards us. I feel her presence before I see her. Porter barely gets his arms uncrossed before the excited blonde jumps towards him.

"You're actually here! I can't believe it!"

He sets her down with a grunt.

"I told you I would."

The woman calms down a little more as she settles under

his arm and faces me. "Hi! You must be Torrance. My brother has told me a lot about you."

I eye an embarrassed Porter. He's talked about me? Interesting.

"Don't believe everything he's told you. I'm sure most of it isn't true," I say, all while looking right at Porter.

"Porter doesn't know how to lie. He's the most honest person I know."

"Torrance, this is my annoying little sister, Zion."

Zion elbows him in the ribs.

"I'm not annoying."

"You are right now, and you said so yourself, I never lie." She elbows him again.

"Nice to meet you.... Wait," things start adding up in my head, "you're Zion?"

She nods.

"You're the one who was texting him all morning?"

"Only because *someone* was ignoring me."

"I told you I was driving," Porter grumbles, but I can see he's only pretending to be exasperated with her. He turns his attention to me, "Wait, who did you think I was getting messages from?"

It's my turn to feel embarrassed. This is the second time today, and I'm not a fan. I clear my throat.

"No one. Your sister. Obviously, because you were."

The look on his face tells me he doesn't believe me, but thankfully he doesn't pursue any more questions on the matter.

Zion squeals again as she hugs him. It's clear she adores him. It's adorable seeing them together. It's fascinating seeing how they interact. They are complete opposites in every way, and yet their love and adoration is evident.

"We should go in and eat! I'm sure you're starving!" Zion exclaims. "Well, maybe not you." She gives her brother a knowing look. "You probably had a protein bar an hour ago or whatever your food schedule is."

I snort. He did in fact have a protein bar not that long ago.

Zion looks over at me, "Do you follow his regimented schedule or are you normal?"

"Why am I here if all you're going to do is make fun of me?" Porter interjects.

"Because you love me."

I laugh. It's something Carson would say.

"Stop making it so easy for her and maybe she would stop," I tease.

Porter's eyes meet mine in challenge, and I find I don't want to look away. A throat clears, causing me to notice the grin on Zion's face. Scrambling for something to say, I end up making some incoherent sound and walking inside the nearby pizza shop.

I see a few more people inside, which gives me hope that there might actually be life in this town after all. "Where is everyone? Isn't this a college town?"

Zion laughs. "This is the old part of town. There are more places the closer to campus you get, but I know how much Porter loves pizza so I thought this would be a better location to meet."

After we order our food, we find a table to sit and visit. Zion tells us all about her classes and some of the campus drama. She tries to involve me as much as possible in the conversation, but I hold back, allowing the siblings time to visit. It's clear they don't get to see each other often. I don't know what I would do if I went almost seven months without seeing Carson. Okay, that's not entirely true. We went that long, sometimes longer when I was in college, but it's been years since we've gone more than a month.

I've been lost in my thoughts and have no idea what Zion just said to me, and by the amused look on Porter's face, I'm guessing she's said it a few times.

"I'm sorry," I apologize. "I must have zoned out. Late night and all."

Zion waves me off. "No need to apologize. I was just saying that you and Porter should totally come to my show tonight!"

She squeals again. I wasn't aware people actually made that sound before today. And I lived with Millie.

"Um," I look over at Porter. Does he want to stay? Is he waiting for me to make the excuse that we need to get back on the road? He's giving me nothing. "What kind of show is it?"

Zion giggles.

"You already talked about that, didn't you?" I ask. How zoned out was I?

"It's okay! I'm singing with my band at a bar and grill near campus tonight. It's kind of a big deal. It's pretty hard to get a gig there, and if things go well, we could get put into their line-up, which would be amazing!"

I look over at Porter again. He's still not giving any indication on what he wants to do. Then I look back at Zion and see how excited she is and how much she wants her big brother to be at her first big gig, and I know what my answer is. We have to stay.

"Of course we should go!" I say with as much excitement as I can. I mean, I love music and bands. And they have to be at least somewhat decent to get the spot in the first place, right?

Porter seems surprised by my answer. Funny how I can read that from his body language, and yet when I was trying to figure out what he wanted me to say I couldn't even get the book open, let alone find the right page to read.

"Are you sure? That would put us on the road pretty late."

I wave my phone at him. "I'm already looking at places to stay that are closer to town. We can get an early morning start and make up time. We already built-in a buffer, so we have plenty of time."

"Yeah, but we don't want to use the entirety of the buffer on the first full day of driving."

"We won't. I'll look for something an hour or two out. It will be late, but it won't be as late as it would be if we went the whole way that we originally planned. It will be fine. Your precious buffer won't be too damaged."

Porter closes his eyes and takes a deep breath. Why is it so fun getting him all annoyed?

"So you'll stay?" Zion looks at her brother with the biggest puppy dog face. She even adds the fake pout.

I sit back, amused as I watch the interaction. He's determined to keep her at bay as long as possible, but eventually he can't hold back his smile as he tells her we will stay. Zion squeals so loudly that multiple heads turn to see what all the commotion is about. Zion is either completely unaware or just doesn't care. Have I mentioned that I really like her?

ZION MAJORLY UNDERSOLD how big of a deal this gig is. This isn't just some local bar and grill; this is the main hang out of the town. There's a line down the street of people trying to get in. The only reason we were able to find a table was because we were with the band. Who knew being a groupie to a band you don't know the name of or any music from would come in handy?

Zion's band is slotted to play second tonight, so I take the time to look for places for us to stay while we listen to the first band. This group is decent enough, but they are trying so hard to be "good" that they don't seem to have their own sound yet. I mean, play covers; you don't need to have original songs or anything, but make the songs your own. This isn't a cover band kind of gig. My inner monologue shifts from Millie's voice telling me to give them a chance to Kiersten's pointing out how they're doing their best and playing really well. Gosh, my friends' sunny optimism can be annoying sometimes. And they aren't even here. This is just what my subconscious is thinking they would say.

"I never said thank you," Porter says between songs.

I look over at him. "For what?"

"For staying. For making me stay. I didn't really want to, but I also didn't want to disappoint Zion. I don't see her too often, and when I do, it's usually when we are back home, so I've never seen her perform."

"Did she not used to sing?"

"Maybe?"

"Is that a question or an answer? Do you not know?"

Porter gives a slight grimace. "We're eight years apart. The last time we lived under the same roof she was eleven, and I was busy trying to earn money for school and help my grandparents around the farm. When I had a spare moment, I mostly tried not to put myself into a panic about what would happen if my mom went out of remission while I was at school. Would I need to drop out? Who would help Zion with her homework? And so on. I didn't pay much attention to anything else."

There's a lot to unpack there. But it's also the most personal information I've ever heard Porter share before. Not that I ever gave him the chance. "I get it. Being the oldest is hard."

What else can I say? I understand, and yet I don't. Our situations are so different. Both my parents were around. They worked a lot, but they were there. And Abuela lived with us, not the other way around. Plus, I had the Jacobsons. Millie's parents, her whole family really, are like a second family to me. They were always there if Carson and I needed anything.

I want to ask more questions, but Zion's band is setting up.

I get an email confirmation for a cute little BnB I found. It's too bad it will be dark when we get there. It looks like they have a beautiful trail that wraps around the property. Maybe I'll get up a little extra early tomorrow and go for a run. If the pictures are anything to go by, I'd hate to miss seeing the scenery.

"We have a place to stay," I tell Porter.

"You found something?"

"Did you think I was going to make us sleep in the car?"

Porter rolls his eyes. I'm starting to notice how much he does that. I just wonder if it's a normal reaction to things, or if it's just me that brings it out of him. "No. I just figured we would end up in some dive motel along the side of the highway."

"A dive motel? Gross." I turn up my nose. "I might not come across as high maintenance, but I have my standards."

"You *might not* come across as high maintenance? I think what you mean to say is you are."

"I am not!"

"You are too. You're a total passenger princess. You have multiple bags of luggage."

"In comparison to what, your one bag? I'm sorry not all of us dress like Harry Potter and only have one shirt to last us all seven years at Hogwarts."

"That was oddly specific."

"How have you not noticed that he wears the same shirt in basically every movie?"

"Because it's a children's movie, and I don't obsess over it."

"I don't obsess! And it's not a children's movie!"

"The books were literally written for children."

"No. They were written for people who like fantasy, and last time I checked that includes children, teens, and adults alike."

"You're the type of person who knows which house you belong to, aren't you?"

"Slytherin. Obviously. And you are the type of person who was too busy with your nose in a book to take a moment to enjoy something because it was fun. Like the Ravenclaw that you are."

Porter starts to say something, but he's interrupted by the announcement of Zion's band.

Queen Zi and the Stripes are good. They have the whole audience engaged. Zion is a natural performer, and it is obvious how much she loves what she is doing, even when she pulled out her guitar and did some acoustic covers to give the rest of the band a breather.

I will admit the most surprising part of the night was when she dragged Porter up on the stage to sing with her. And I do mean dragged. Even after the short amount of time I have spent with him this weekend I can tell how uncomfortable he was being in front of all those people. At first he tried to refuse, but being a younger sibling she knew just the right buttons to push and soon had the whole crowd cheering for him to come up on stage. She handed him her guitar, and as soon as he hit the first chord, it was as if he was replaced by someone else. She got him to sing two songs with her. When I say that man can sing, I mean he can *sing*! Who knew?

When Porter comes back down to the table, I'm gawking at him.

"What?" Porter asked sheepishly.

"You can sing," I say, dumbfounded.

"Yeah…?"

"And play the guitar," I again state the obvious.

"Yes."

"How did I not know this about you?" I mean, I know why; I have never tried to get to know Porter. He was a jerk the first time we met, and that was it. I have been judging him for it ever since.

"I don't really broadcast it. I don't think Duncan even knows."

"You lived together."

Porter nods.

"For years."

He nods again.

"How did he never find out?"

"I didn't have a guitar with me at school, and I don't exactly go around singing to myself all the time."

I'm glad it's darker in here so he can't see my blush. I do go around singing all the time. Loudly. At least I do when I'm not at work. If a song pops in my head, I sing it.

Porter must see something in my expression because he adds, "Not that it's a bad thing to do. I didn't mean to insinuate anything."

He's nervously babbling. Normally I would enjoy this, but after everything I've learned about him tonight, I decide to let him off the hook.

"Porter, it's fine. I know I'm loud. I've been told my whole life I'm loud and abrasive." I shrug. "I've just come to terms with it, and it is what it is. I try, albeit not hard enough at times, to be less, but it never seems to stick."

Porter's expression shifts from embarrassment to something that looks like concern. "You should never have to lessen yourself, Torrance. Anyone worth anything isn't worth losing yourself over."

I have a feeling there is more to that statement than what we've been talking about, but I appreciate it all the same.

"Thank you. That means a lot. Especially coming from you."

"Especially coming from me?"

"Don't know if you've noticed or not, but we don't exactly have the greatest track record for getting along."

"Oh, I don't know. I think we've done pretty well the last couple of days."

"Two days in eight years isn't that great of a track record."

"It's also the longest we've spent together in those eight years. And definitely the most isolated we've ever been."

He has a point, but it also makes me wonder if we will go back to how things have always been once we are with everyone again. I can't believe I'm even thinking this, but I kind of hope not. I like the guy sitting next to me. The one who, even though he didn't want to, got up on stage and sang with his sister. The guy who my niece liked enough to give a nickname. There are a lot more layers to Porter Collins than my stubborn self ever noticed. As much as I pride myself on being a pretty good judge of character, I'm starting to think everything I ever thought about Porter was wrong.

CHAPTER 21

Porter

I DON'T KNOW WHAT I was expecting from our visit with my sister, but tonight wasn't it. I was furious that Zi called me up on stage like that. And I know she did it from the stage so I wouldn't be able to say no, because that is just who my sister is. She knows I hate being the center of attention, a trait we clearly don't share, but I would do anything for her, and she also knows that.

Have to admit, no matter how surprised I was about my sister's talent, the thing I was most surprised about was Torrance. It feels like for the first time we had a real conversation. It wasn't laced with sarcasm or ended in some joke. It was a real conversation that felt like we got to know one another.

It's late when we finally leave Zion, and even later when we make it to the BnB Torrance found online. Torrance is curled up in her seat asleep when we pull up. I hate to disturb her, but the woman who owns the place is staying up for us to arrive. Torrance had called her when we were on our way to let her know we would be later than originally planned.

"Hey, Tor," I gently shake her shoulder. She groans but otherwise doesn't move.

"Torrance, we're here," I say as I brush her now-messy curls from her face. She looks so beautiful and peaceful.

Torrance's eyes flutter open as my hand is mid-swipe. "We're stopped."

I sit back in my seat and smile. "Yeah, we are."

"How long have you been trying to wake me up?" she asks as she sits up.

"Not long, I just parked."

Torrance opens her door and stretches. It takes everything in me not to let my eyes linger on the strip of skin between her jeans and tank top. I groan inwardly. What am I doing? I can't have these thoughts and feelings about Torrance. She hates me. And I'm not her biggest fan. Though those two things might not be quite as true anymore. We have definitely gotten to know each other more the last few days. As much as I know my opinion has changed, I'm not certain about hers. I'm pretty confident she doesn't completely hate me anymore so I guess that is something. But what hasn't changed is that she's loud, and chaos follows wherever she goes. I meant what I said earlier that she should never make herself less to please others, but I also know that I can't deal with that. I like my quiet and predictable life. It's stable and, for lack of a better word, predictable. I thrive on my routine where Torrance seems to thrive in mayhem.

"Porter, are you coming? Or are you planning on sleeping out here tonight?" Torrance questions, but while once she would have had an annoyed tone, now she just sounds amused.

I clear my throat. "Yeah. Why don't I get our bags, and you get us checked in since you're the one who's talked to her?"

"Sounds good."

Torrance is much more awake now and bounds up the steps towards the front door. I take a moment to calm my racing heart. What is going on? It's not like I never noticed how beautiful she is. I've always recognized that, even if it was reluctantly.

The first time Duncan and I went over to the girls' apartment after the ill-fated skate party, I was completely taken by her, but the damage had already been done. I was the jerk that had knocked her down and nothing I could ever do would change that. I spent most of the night getting glared at—that is, when she even acknowledged my existence. I get it, I was a jerk that first night. I had a migraine and didn't feel well. I never should have gone. I understood that, but it didn't matter how much I tried to apologize, she wouldn't give me the chance.

That second night pretty much set up the pattern for the last eight years. I'd get dragged somewhere I didn't want to be; Torrance ignored me as much as possible. I'd sit back and watch her. At first I was intrigued, then I was mad she wouldn't get over the skate debacle or at least let me say I was sorry, until finally, I was just annoyed. I started going out of my way to get under her skin. If she wanted to dislike me, then fine. Two could play that game.

I need to shake off all thoughts of the past. Dwelling on what's already happened isn't going to get me anywhere. I'm too in my head. I just need to get into my room and wash off this long day and get some sleep. Nothing a long hot shower and a good night's sleep can't fix.

IT'S CURRENTLY 5:00 AM, and I've been up since 2:00. Considering we didn't get checked into our rooms until after 11:00, it's safe to say sleep did not fix all my problems. Apparently, the fact that Torrance's room was directly to the left of mine and these walls are entirely too thin was too much for my brain. All I could do was think of the feisty woman on the other side of the wall. I need out of this room.

I pull out my running clothes from my bag. Might as well get in some exercise before being trapped in the car all day with the one thing my brain can't seem to stop thinking about. This is longer than I usually go without working out, but there hasn't been time.

The morning air is still crisp, and there is a slight breeze. Looking up at the sky, it seems like a storm is on its way. I just hope we can get in front of it and that it's moving the opposite direction from us.

One last stretch and I'm off. Each pounding step of my feet on the pavement gives me a little more clarity. That is, until I see something neon orange up ahead. I don't even have to look closely to know who it is. She must hear me coming up behind her since Torrance stops and waits for me to catch up.

"You're up early." Torrance is barely out of breath as she speaks. I, on the other hand, keep taking big gulps of air in order to not gasp, but I'm pretty sure it's because of the woman standing in front of me and not the run.

Torrance adjusts her sports bra, and I divert my eyes. I had been blissfully unaware of what exactly she was wearing, and now it's a shock wave to my brain. I really need her to put on some more clothes. Perhaps even a parka. Actually, yes, a parka. That would cover every single curve and slope of her body.

I clear my throat, which feels far too dry. "Couldn't sleep."

"That makes sense." It does? I'm about to say something incriminating when she continues, "You work mostly nights, right? Being awake during the day and sleeping at night would feel weird."

"Umm, yeah." That isn't it at all, but I'm grateful for the easy out. "What about you? I thought you didn't like mornings."

Torrance shrugs. "I don't. I saw pictures of this trail on the website when I was booking the room, and I wanted to see it before we left. I'm also used to being up before the sun so I can get in a run before work."

"Why not just run after work?"

"Sometimes I do that too. I usually have something going on with roommates or friends, so mornings just work better. Besides, it makes my workday go smoother."

There is some hidden meaning behind that, and it makes me want to know more. It has nothing to do with the woman who is claiming every space of my brain. I am just a curious guy.

"You don't like where you work?"

"I didn't say that," she says defensively.

Way to go, Porter. Things have been cordial for the last few days so now I have to open my stupid mouth and ruin it.

There is just a look about her that makes my old habit of arguing with her snap right back into place.

"It was just a question. No need to bite my head off," I retort. And I know I shouldn't react, but why does she get to be defensive and mad at me? All I did was ask a question.

"No need to get so snooty," Torrance shoots back. "I'll just let you get back to your run."

And with that she turns and takes off, leaving me with my proverbial foot in my mouth while simultaneously kicking myself. I give her a few minutes' head start and then continue. I could go faster, but I have a feeling if I run into Torrance again, things won't go any smoother. Best to give her space while I can.

CHAPTER 22

Torrance

ORTER JUST MAKES me so mad! Just when I thought we were actually going to get along on this trip, he had to be...he's just so... I don't even know. He just...is!

I continue running down the small winding road, pushing myself faster and faster. I should probably take it easy since I took a couple extra days off while visiting Valley Creek, but I'm just irritated enough to not care how tired I'll be later. Maybe this way I'll sleep in the car and then not have to talk to Porter.

A couple miles later, I come to a fork in the road and decide it would be best if I head back. Knowing me I'll get lost, and then there would be one more thing I'll get criticized for by the ever-perfect Porter. Though I have to admit in hindsight, he didn't really say anything demeaning or rude earlier. I didn't have to bite his head off. He just hit way too close to the mark. I don't really like my job. I mean, I like what I do, and I like most of who I work with, but over all? No. I don't like my job. Frankly I do a whole lot of babysitting of Walter Wade's grown adult children. I went into human resources because I like helping people reach their potential, and I like being able to stand up for the guy who's low on the totem pole. Carson says I have a hero complex, but I like to think of it as more of a big sister mentality.

Growing up, we didn't exactly have a lot of people in our corner. Those we had were more than enthusiastic, but there weren't many. Mom and Dad are great, and I love them with every fiber of my being. They just put a lot of focus on work. They made a lot of sacrifices for us to live where we did so we could go to the schools that we did. And they did that so we would have the opportunities that they never had growing up. I get that. It just would have been nice to have parents who showed up to my concerts or came to the plays that I designed sets for. Millie's family was more than happy to adopt me into their fold, but it wasn't the same. Norah and Dan Jacobson are fantastic people, but they aren't Rafael and Nichelle Rodriguez. The only member of my family that was there day in and day out for me was my sister, but I'm the older sister. It's my job to be there for her. I like to think I've done that. Sometimes not as much as I wish, like when she married that weasel after graduation, but without that spoiled jerk, we wouldn't have Aly.

My thoughts continue to spiral as I run back towards the BnB. I guess my usual over-thinking and insomniac ways are going to continue this trip. I was really hopeful that they weren't. I have slept so well the last few days. Up until last night when I couldn't stop thinking about Porter.

He's so different than I perceived him to be. All the new information I learned yesterday made a lot of things make sense. Which set me on edge because I know I've been wrong to judge him as I have and to treat him as I have. Then he made his comment about me not liking my job, and I lost it. I just need things to go back to normal. Back to when I couldn't stand him. I know how to operate life that way. I've had eight years of practice not liking Porter Collins. I don't know how to operate in a world where I not only don't think he's so bad, but one where I think I could actually like him. Which is just ridiculous.

I need to get back to the BnB and then shower and find food. That will fix everything. Or at the very least put a bandaid on it so I can ignore it some more.

NEWS FLASH: A shower and food did not, in fact, fix everything. It didn't make things worse, but it fixed nothing. I still can't shake the feeling of needing to apologize to Porter, which I know seems simple, but it's not. I hate having to apologize; it makes me feel weak. I hate having to admit that I was in the wrong. The only people I'm even remotely good at apologizing to are Millie and Jonathan, and even then, it's not like I've had enough practice. Jonathan just gets me, so when we argue, it usually just ends up getting shrugged off. And I do the same with him.

Millie is just so happy and positive that it takes a lot to get her riled up. Like a few months ago, she and her now-husband, Mark, had been hiding their relationship from their families, which meant she kept it from Jonathan, and it was kind of a mess when it came out. She and I had been at odds because I thought she should tell Jonathan, since Mark is his brother, and it kind of got between us. But when Jonathan blew up at her, she was miserable. I went into fix-it mode, which led to a long heart-to-heart. Turns out she had been feeling a little over-shadowed. Which I of course felt terrible about. The last thing I would ever want is for one of my friends to feel like their opinion doesn't matter. Or that their voice isn't heard. I still don't feel like my apology was adequate enough, but she forgave me anyway. Because Millie Jacobson, well, I guess technically it's Winters now, can't stay mad for long.

Maybe part of what's been bothering me is that everyone seems to be moving on with their lives. Millie is a Winters now. She and Jonathan aren't just best friends anymore. They're in-laws. Our trio is more of a duo. I know they've been friends since birth, but I never felt left out. It's always been the three of us, but since Millie and Mark got together, things have shifted. First it was Jonathan being kind of a jerk about it, which put me in the awkward position of being in the middle, but then when it all got resolved, they became literal family. While I'm still just the best friend. But Jonathan and I aren't Millie's best friends anymore, Mark is. As it should be. They're married. She should be completely obsessed and in love with her husband. I might not do relationships, but if I did, that's the only kind I could do.

I just feel left behind.

Now Amara and Duncan are getting married. Which I still haven't fully accepted. I know I'm on this road trip because of their engagement, but I still feel like there is the possibility it won't happen. It took them eight years to get to this point; maybe I have another eight years before they go the rest of the way. What am I even saying? I don't want that for Amara. I want her to be happy, and if Duncan makes her happy, then good for her. It has nothing to do with me. See what I mean? I get so in my head about feeling left out that I turn into this selfish being who hopes that her friend's happiness gets postponed, so I don't feel as left out.

Man, I need help! Maybe I should make an appointment with the therapist Wade hired last year to help boost company morale as an initiative towards positive mental health.

Then again, going to a therapist at work and complaining about said work environment probably isn't the best idea. Maybe I should find someone outside the office?

I'm in the middle of my debate when there is a knock on my door. I open it to find a slightly annoyed Porter. I totally deserve that attitude. Though I also know I shouldn't just assume it's about me. At least not all about me. Non-self-centered thoughts, Tori. You got this.

"Come on in," I move to give him space to enter. He hesitates but ends up coming in.

"I was just coming to see if you were ready to get on the road. We have about an eight hour drive ahead of us today since we took that detour yesterday."

Old Tori would point out that the detour was his doing, but New Tori knows that it was my idea for us to stay and see his sister's band play. And it was me who found the BnB that took us even further out of the way, even if only by a few miles.

"I just finished packing up my stuff. We can head out whenever you're ready."

Porter nods. "Leave in 10 minutes or so, then?"

"Sounds good." Now would be the perfect time to apologize for this morning, but I'm a coward and don't. I just let Porter grunt at my response and leave the room.

PORTER'S MOOD ISN'T any better when I meet him at the car. I know what I have to do. As much as I would love to put it off, I can't be in a car with this man for the whole day with this demeanor. Not when I know I don't have to.

"Here. Let me take it," Porter takes my bags.

"Thanks." I take one more breath to sum up the courage to apologize and blurt, "I'm sorry about this morning."

Porter's head snaps up to meet my gaze. "What?"

I know he heard me just fine, but I'm not going to let my annoyance get the better of me. That's what got me in this situation in the first place. "I'm sorry I snapped at you. You were just—"

"I was just what, Torrance?" He snaps.

"As I was trying to say," I spit out, "all you were doing was asking a follow-up question, and it hit a little too close to home, and I snapped. It had nothing to do with you, and I'm sorry."

"It's fine."

"Clearly it's not."

"I said it's fine, and it is. We should get going."

"No." I refuse to get into the car until this is resolved.

"Just get in the car, Torrance," Porter's annoyance is building with every moment, but I still refuse to budge.

"No." I don't know what else to do so I sit down. Right there on the dirt road next to the car. This red dirt will probably stain my perfectly good denim shorts, but I don't care. I'm too stubborn to give up now.

Porter groans. "Are you seriously just going to sit there?"

"Yes."

"Your clothes are going to get stained."

Ha. Joke's on him, I already thought of that. "I know. I'm not moving until you agree to accept my apology."

He runs a hand over his face and looks up to the sky before looking back down at me. "I already told you it was fine."

"Yes, but I don't believe you. And I'm not moving until I believe that you really do accept my apology. So I'm going to say it one more time. Porter, I'm sorry I got snappy with you this morning. It was uncalled for. Your question hit a little too close to home, but that doesn't mean it was a warranted response."

Porter paces for a bit with his hands on his hips all while I sit crisscross in the dirt. He finally stops right in front of me and crouches down so that we are more or less eye to eye. "I accept your apology and issue one of my own."

He has my interest.

"When I noticed that I hit a nerve, I should have let it go. I didn't need to snap back at you."

"Truce?" I stick my hand out, but Porter doesn't take it.

"I think we need something stronger than a truce. We've already made and broken several."

"Fine." I take back my outstretched hand and offer up my pinky.

"A pinky promise?" Porter's eyebrow raises in suspicion.

"You said we needed something stronger than a truce," I say matter-of-factly. "It was either this or a blood oath, and frankly that seems a little excessive... and messy. Plus I don't have a knife."

There's a hint of amusement, but Porter eventually takes my pinky in his. "Pinky promise it is."

In one swift movement, Porter releases my pinky, wraps his hand around my wrist, and pulls me to my feet. His hand is more callused than I was expecting, and the strength behind it makes my knees wobble a little. Lucky for me, I can play it off as losing my balance. Porter helps right me then lets go, but only after I swear he glances at my mouth for a beat. I must be imagining things. The lack of sleep is getting to me... right?

I dust myself off as I head to the passenger side of the car.

"Do you want to drive?" Porter's question surprises me. This thing is a boat. It's huge. Not to mention it belongs to Trent. His cousin. I haven't seen Trent, other than on a cereal box or toothpaste commercial, since high school.

"Why?"

"Why, what?"

"Why are you asking if I want to drive?" I ask him. We might have just pinky promised to get along, but that doesn't mean I want him to just give me what he thinks I want.

"Don't read into it, Torrance. I'm not just giving in to you for the sake of giving in. I was just curious if you wanted to drive at all."

Can he read my mind, or did I say some of that out loud?

"I drive a Jeep," is all I can manage to say. As if what I drive is the only explanation that's needed as to why I would never want to drive Trent's Escalade.

Porter's face scrunches in confusion. "What does you driving a Jeep have anything to do with this?"

It's a fair question.

"This thing is way too big. I'm not driving this monstrosity."

Porter doesn't even try to hide his smirk this time. "Okay."

We finally get settled into the car and head back towards the highway.

"So what music do you have for us today?"

I smile over at Porter, "See, I told you I'd win you over."

Porter laughs. "I never said you won me over. I still like audiobooks and silence; I just know that you are more pleasant when you have music playing."

I can't help the laugh that bubbles out of me. "Oh, and here I thought we were going to get along."

"We are. You want music. You get music. I don't want to hear you complain about the music. I put you in charge of the music. Simply surviving over here."

I laugh but hook up my phone and start today's playlist.

CHAPTER 23

Porter

WE'RE SEVERAL HOURS into our drive today when Torrance starts rustling through her bag. Suddenly, she's unbuckling her seatbelt and all but crawling into the back seat. I try to keep my eyes on the road and see what she is doing at the same time. All while not focusing on her bare midriff that is getting dangerously close to my face. She's invading my space in all ways possible, making it hard to concentrate on the road ahead when her hip hits my shoulder causing me to jostle.

"What are you doing?" Not really a fan of a shrill sound that just escaped my mouth, but we're in a moving vehicle and she's acting like we're parked.

Torrance slides back into her seat with a triumphant gleam in her eye. "Grabbing this."

She shakes what looks like a large tackle box.

"What is it?" I'm still annoyed at her blatant disregard for safety.

"My snacklebox."

"Your what?!"

"My snacklebox. It was in the bag Millie gave me." Her matter-of-fact tone is really grating on my nerves.

"You risked your life for a snack?!"

"Will you relax? I didn't risk my life."

"You were hanging halfway in the back of the car while it was moving!"

"Yeah, and nothing happened, so relax."

"Just because nothing happened doesn't mean it couldn't have. There are rules and laws for a reason."

"Well, I was hungry, and I'm pretty sure there's a rule about that too."

I eye her.

"I'm assuming Millie gave you a list of rules and guidelines about traveling with me."

"It was a whole binder," I grit out.

"Why am I not surprised," Torrance sighs. "Well, if there was a binder then I'm sure there is a whole section on not letting me travel hungry."

"I haven't read it," I admit.

Torrance laughs. "You're either very brave or very stupid."

I'm thinking it's more of the latter at the moment.

Torrance proceeds to open up her box of snacks. I give it a brief glance and see nothing but bright artificial coloring. Gummies of every shape and size, M&Ms, Skittles, and I'm pretty sure I even see some mini marshmallows.

"So you're just going to sit and eat a bunch of junk?"

"Don't worry, I'll share. But you have to ask nicely."

"No, thanks. I prefer not to eat junk food."

"It's not all junk food," Torrance mocks. "See." She starts digging into the bottom layer of the box. "There are some pretzels, trail mix, jerky, and— gross! Why did she put those in here?"

I can't help it; my interest is peeked. "What is it?"

"Yogurt covered raisins."

I roll my eyes.

"Want anything?"

"Not really."

"Oh, come on. You can't have a road trip without snacks. It's like the law."

"Actually, it's not."

"Do you have to be so matter-of-fact all the time? Food can be for more than just to fuel your body, you know. You can enjoy what you are eating once in a while. Don't think I haven't noticed how healthy you've been eating. Loosen up, Porter. It's just a snack. A pack of Skittles isn't going to ruin your six-pack."

"Who said I have a six-pack?" I do, but how does she know that? I have never been shirtless anywhere near Torrance in all eight years we have known each other.

"Oh, please. You're the classic workaholic, much too serious, exercises every day to 'relieve stress' kind of guy."

"What's with the air quotes around 'relieve stress'?"

Torrance laughs again, and as much as I like the sound, I'm not particularly fond of it being directed at me. "Because no matter how much you try to convince yourself and others that you don't care what people think about you, you really do care. And while I think you want to be healthy and are a bit of a health nut, I'm also at least 75% sure you don't totally hate when attractive women like what they see. You forget, I've known you for a long time."

She thinks she has me all figured out. Well, she's wrong. Or mostly wrong. I do like to exercise and eat healthy, but it has nothing to do with how I look and everything to do with trying to be as healthy as possible. I've seen firsthand how quickly life can change, and I want to do everything in my power to be the best I can be with however much time I'm allotted on this earth.

It's time for a subject change. I don't really care to hear any more speculations about what Torrance thinks my life is like.

"You mentioned you drive a Jeep? I didn't peg you as an outdoorsy kind of person."

"I'm not."

"But you drive a Jeep."

"Yes," she drawls out. "That doesn't mean I fit into the stereotype. I just liked the car, so I bought it. Plus, it's orange."

There's more to that story. I glance over at her. "So you picked your car purely for the color?"

I mean it's plausible. She is definitely the type of person to base such a big decision on something so trivial.

"Well, no," she stammers. "But you'll make fun of me for the real reason, and I don't feel like getting made fun of at the moment so we're going to go with it."

"You just roasted me on my healthy eating habits, I think you owe me."

I don't expect that to work, but she answers, "Have you heard of ducking?"

"Excuse me?"

"Ducking. It's when Jeep drivers give other Jeep drivers rubber ducks." She shifts in her seat to face me better. "Okay, let's say you see a Jeep, and you like the color or a sticker or something that they have, so to let them know you leave a rubber duck on their door handle. When you receive a duck, you display it on the dashboard. I have a whole basket of ducks in my backseat. I'm a bit of a rebel and only keep the ones I really like on my dashboard. And I tend to trade them out often. I keep those in a separate basket. Don't want to accidentally give away a duck I want to keep."

"So you learned about ducking and decided you had to have a Jeep. I can see why that would be embarrassing," I say dryly.

Torrance rolls her eyes. "That's not the embarrassing part." She takes a deep breath. "Have you ever seen the movie *Pretty in Pink*?"

"The old brat pack movie?"

"Yes, well, it's my favorite movie. And I love Duckie, you know, Jon Cryer's character?"

I snort. "Are you telling me you picked your vehicle, that you drive every single day, based off of a game that is played with said vehicle owners based on the fact that it shares similarities with a nickname to a fictional character?"

"I told you it was embarrassing!"

"It's not that bad." I try to keep a straight face, but as soon as I see her glare, I burst out laughing. "Okay, it's pretty bad."

"Shut up." Torrance shoves my arm, but she's laughing too.

Torrance covers her face, but I can still see a slight tint of pink to her tan skin. It takes everything out of me to keep my focus on the road ahead of us.

"I need a topic change!" Torrance announces. Out of

my periphery, I see her straighten in her seat. "What's a hidden talent you have that most people wouldn't know about you?"

"I don't have any hidden talents."

"Oh, come on! Up until last night I had no idea you played the guitar. And you can sing!"

"That's not a hidden talent."

"You said yourself that not even Duncan knows about it, so that's a hidden talent."

"Okay, then that one."

Torrance harrumphs. "If we're going to play the game, then I'm going to need you to actually play along."

"Now it's a game? Fine, what's your hidden talent?"

"I asked you first!"

"I asked you second," I retort.

I expect her to put up more of a fight, but instead she answers, "I know every word to 'We Didn't Start the Fire'."

I give her a skeptical look. "Like the song?"

"Yes, like the song."

"Prove it." She could spout off a bunch of nonsense, and I wouldn't know the difference, but I know asking her to sing the song will give me time to come up with an answer.

Torrance finishes her song, and I give a mock round of applause. No idea how accurate she was, but she definitely had a lot of words spitting out quickly to the melody.

"Now, what's yours? Or do you need me to sing another song so you can come up with one?" She looks at me in challenge. Busted.

"Um, I don't know if it's a talent or not, but I know the capital of every state."

"Okay, prove it. But unlike you, I'm going to check your work." She grabs her phone and starts typing.

"It's a little hard to fact check while driving." I give her a quick glance.

"Let's see. What is the capital of…" she starts mumbling to herself. "Not that one. Everyone knows that one. Umm…" Finally, she decides which state to start with. "Okay, Smart Guy, what's the capital of Iowa?"

She's taking this all so seriously, I can't help but mess with her. "I."

"I?"

"The capital of Iowa is I."

Torrance huffs out a breath. "Really?"

I can't contain my smile. "Sorry, you were just being so serious. I couldn't help myself."

"Cute," she says sarcastically.

"So you've said." My eyes go wide for the briefest of seconds when I realize what I've said. Before she has a chance to connect any dots, I add, "The capital of Iowa is Des Moines."

She looks at her phone. "Correct."

We go back and forth for a few more states.

New Hampshire: Concord.

Maine: Augusta.

North Dakota: Bismarck.

I wasn't kidding when I said I know all of them. It was something I learned when I was a kid, and it just stuck in my head. I can name every US president in order too, but Torrance doesn't need to know just how big of a nerd I was as a kid…or still am.

"So where are we staying tonight?"

"At this little BnB that I found. The town looks so cute online, and they are having a festival this week which just sounded like fun."

"You really like bed and breakfasts, don't you?"

"What do you mean?"

"I mean we stayed at one last night. Now this place. I was just noticing how you haven't booked any hotels."

"BnBs are just, I don't know. I like how they feel more like a home. Hotels are so sterile and void of any personality. My parents used to work out of town a lot, and sometimes Carson and I would go with them. We always got so bored. Then a few years ago my roommates and I went on a trip, and we stayed at the cutest bed and breakfast, and I was hooked."

"That makes sense. I'm assuming we will be staying at BnBs exclusively then?"

"Until we get to Amara's grandparents."

We follow the GPS for a few more minutes before we pull up to a circular gravel driveway. We park in the designated spots and take the walkway to the front door. This place is definitely more eclectic than where we stayed last night. I'm almost scared to walk through the doors if the porch decorations are any indication of what we will find inside.

SITTING IN MY room, I'm still a little overwhelmed as I take in the apple orchard décor. Apparently each room in this place is themed after a different fruit. And when I say themed, I mean themed. There's a full mural of an apple tree with actual branches protruding from the wall creating a canopy effect over the bed. There are baskets of faux apples all over the place. Even the soap in the bathroom is apple scented.

The woman who owns this place was very polite, almost too polite, if I'm honest. I swear she would have talked until she got our entire back stories, but thankfully Torrance intercepted and started asking questions about the festival going on downtown.

Torrance and I decide to meet up in an hour to head downtown and check it all out. We both need a break from the car. I can't speak for Torrance, but I also need a break from her.

After our rocky start this morning, I wasn't sure how the day was going to go, but it ended up being the best day we've ever had. And that's kind of a problem. I know how to deal with things when she's mad at me. I've even navigated us getting along for periods of time, but today was different. She was different. It's like I saw the real Torrance for the first time. I don't even know how to explain it, but the woman I was in the car with today is someone I could very easily lose my heart to. I'm just not sure I know how to do that, or even if I want to. When it comes to my parents, I didn't exactly have the strongest example of what it means to stay in a relationship. I mean, sure, my grandparents are built on longevity, and they more than helped raise me and Zion. But it's different. They are from a different time. They grew up together. They were high school sweethearts. She waited for him while he served in the army. They got married and never looked back. Even through grief and tragedy.

I just need to take a power nap. Maybe that will help clear my head?

GUESS I WAS more tired than I thought I was. I wake up with a start as I hear knocking at my door. I wipe the sleep from my eyes as I answer the door with a yawn.

"Did I wake you up?"

I look at Torrance, all bright-eyed and relaxed. Maybe it's still the sleep fog, but she's breathtaking even in a t-shirt and jeans.

"I was just resting my eyes."

"I can go by myself if you want to rest. I'm sure you're exhausted after driving all day."

It might be wishful thinking, but it doesn't feel like she wants to go by herself. And I don't want her to either. Not that this is a date or anything, but I feel kind of responsible for her. I mean, we don't know this place or these people. What's the crime rate? Is this place even safe? I know Torrance is more than capable of taking care of herself; I'm not delusional. I would just feel better knowing I was there in case something did happen. Trent makes fun of me for always being such a pessimist, but unlike him, I don't live in a world full of sunshine and rainbows. There are some scary and dangerous things out there. So, yes. I am going with Torrance tonight, you know, for safety. No other reason.

"I just need to put shoes on."

Torrance comes into my room as I walk over to the bed where I had kicked my shoes off. It feels intimate having her in my space like this. I know she's just standing in the room, but it's where I'll sleep tonight.

"Freya said that downtown is only a couple blocks away if you're cool walking."

"That's fine."

"What's wrong?"

"Nothing."

"You look confused."

"I was just wondering who Freya is."

"The woman who owns the bed and breakfast. We met her when we checked in," Torrance says with amusement.

"Got it." I stand up. "Ready?"

We walk the couple of blocks to the center of downtown, and when they say that they go all out for the town peach festival, they weren't kidding. There are peaches everywhere. Peach cobbler, peach ice cream, peach lemonade, peach jam, peach you name it, they got it.

"Where do you want to start?" I ask.

"How about we walk around a bit while we find some dinner? I'm starving."

"Lead the way."

As we walk around, it's clear to see just how much this town is obsessed with peaches. Torrance buys a "Just Peachy" shirt and somehow convinces me to get one as well. I have zero intention of wearing it. We stop at the high school booster club's table for some chili, which is where things start to take a turn.

We barely finished eating when Torrance starts coughing. Her tongue starts to swell, and her body is covered in hives. I need to get her to a hospital. Fast.

♡♡

"ARE YOU THE one who came in with Miss Rodriguez?" The nurse asks.

I follow her back towards the room where Torrance is laying on the bed. Good news is the swelling has majorly gone down. I don't know what she is allergic to, but I'm guessing she should probably have an EpiPen with her from now on. I enter the room, and that's when I notice that Torrance is singing, but I can't quite tell what it is. When she sees me, she sits up with arms open wide.

"Po!"

The singing gets louder, and that's when I finally recognize it.

I look at the nurse. "Is she singing the Teletubbies theme song?

The woman doesn't even try to hide her amusement. "Yep, for the last fifteen minutes. This is the first time she's actually gotten all of their names right though."

Wonderful.

"What is she on? She's pretty out of it."

"Our standard protocol: epinephrine when she first arrived and Benadryl about twenty minutes ago."

"Benadryl did that?" I ask in horror.

You hear stories of how Benadryl has been known to make people loopy and hyper, but it's so rare that I never thought I'd witness it. But of course Torrance is one of those people, because why wouldn't she be? The only thing about Torrance that is predictable is that she's unpredictable.

"And Po!" Torrance yells again.

Not wanting her to cause any more of a scene than she already has in this small-town emergency room, I walk over to her bed. "Hi, Torrance."

"Did you know they put peaches in the chili?"

She's not making any sense.

"The chili?" I ask. Is this more of her delusion?

"Yeah. That chili at the festival. The one I had to force you to try." I start to answer, but she waves me off. "Well, apparently when they say peach festival, they mean it because they put it in the chili! And guess who's allergic to peaches?" She points to herself.

I know for a fact that we haven't been here long enough to do any sort of test that would tell her she's allergic to peaches. This is something she already knew.

"Torrance, do you have a food allergy?" I know we made a pinky promise to get along and we've done a really good job at keeping it today, but that still doesn't stop the annoyance that creeps in. I don't care how out of it she is. She has a known food allergy, one that caused her to have a serious reaction, and she still just tried food like there was no tomorrow.

"Stone fruit," she says matter-of-factly. "Guess I should have brought my EpiPen with me."

"You have a…"

Of all the things she has put me through, this…this has to be the worst of them all. She has a severe food allergy that requires an EpiPen and yet she still insisted we go to a festival that was themed around *the food she is allergic to*! Not only that, but she also still ate food? Without asking questions!

I try to school my features, but even delusional Torrance isn't fooled. "Aww, Po is mad at me! Come here, Po!"

She opens her arms up over her head again. When I don't lean in any closer, she starts to chant again. I lean in to stop the chanting. I am relieved that she is okay, but this woman is something else. As soon as I think I've figured her out even a little, she sends me in a completely different direction. It's exhausting trying to keep up.

Torrance wraps her arms around my middle and gives a tight squeeze. I take a deep breath and relax a bit. She really scared me tonight. I don't know what I would have done if things had gone worse. I mean, having a full on allergic reaction is pretty bad, but it could have been so much worse.

I should probably call her sister and at least Millie so they know what happened. I'll do that as soon as I get her back to her room and in bed. She's going to need some extra sleep tonight. Depending on how she's feeling in the morning, we might need to take some extra time tomorrow. I'm glad that we had the foresight to build in an extra day to get to Nashville. I have a feeling we're going to need it.

I'm still in panic planning mode when the nurse comes in with the discharge papers. I'm to keep an eye on Torrance and call if I have any questions. And if it wasn't evident enough that we are in a small town, the doctor gave me his cell phone number in case there are any complications or if she has another flare up. Otherwise, we are good to go.

Who knew getting a loopy, singing, and, quite frankly, handsy Torrance into the car would be the easy part of the evening? As soon as we are back at the BnB, I help her into her room, which ironically is peach themed. I head to my room to get a change of clothes and an extra blanket and pillow. Looks like I will be sleeping on the floor tonight. Not exactly the most comfortable way to sleep, but I will feel much better being able to constantly watch her rather than sitting and worrying about her between checks while I'm in my room. I grab Millie's binder because I might as well have something to read while I'm on babysitting duty. I'm actually glad Torrance is so out of it because she would hate how much fuss I'm putting into checking on her.

When I walk back into her room, the singing has subsided, and I think she has finally fallen asleep when out of nowhere she shoots up in her bed and glares at me.

"Po."

There's a warning in her voice, but I'm more focused her continually calling me Po. I really hope this isn't something that's going to stick. First her niece calls me Potato, and now I'm a Teletubby. As someone who never had a nickname growing up, it feels weird to be called something other than my name, but if I had to choose, I think I prefer the vegetable.

"Torrance."

She points at me accusingly. "You. Here!"

She points next to her. I really don't want to go over to the bed, but this BnB is very old, and I can only imagine how thin the walls are. We don't need to make any more of a scene in this town than we already have in the last six hours.

I step next to the bed when suddenly Torrance's hands are all over me. I try to grab her hands, but I swear she's growing extra arms.

"What are you, an octopus?!"

"You never showed me your TV!"

Come again?

"You never showed me the TV on your stomach!" She yells as she finally gets a hold of my shirt hem and lifts it.

I try not to shudder, the sensation wracking through my body as her hands explore up and down my abdomen. My skin is on fire everywhere she touches. I can't step away, and I can't look away from her assessing gaze. I can't tell what is going on in her head. Clearly she's still out of it, but she has to know at least on some level what she's doing, right?

After a moment, her roaming slows. It's more agonizing than the quicker pace. Now I'm even more aware of how she is tracing each and every abdominal muscle. She pulls away then looks up at me with an annoyed look on her face. "That's not a TV, Po, that's a freaking remote!"

I fight back a smile. This whole situation is ridiculous, and it's been a long day.

"Sorry to disappoint you."

Torrance huffs as she lays back down, falling asleep quickly. I settle into the chair and watch her as she sleeps.

If I thought it was distracting trying to sleep on the opposite side of the wall from her, it's downright impossible with her mere feet away. Especially as I try to ignore all the thoughts that swim through my head as I replay the way she looked as she roamed her hands up and down my torso. Even the thought of it makes me feel the fire of her skin against mine.

It's going to be a long night, and an even longer remainder of this trip. I have no idea what I'm going to do about these feelings or the woman who's softly snoring from her bed next to me.

CHAPTER 24

Torrance

WHEN I WAKE up, it takes me a minute to figure out where I am. I have a limited memory of what happened yesterday, but what fragments I do have make me want to burrow deep in this bed and hide. I remember eating dinner and then having an allergic reaction. Why didn't I think to check the food? I was so careful not to eat anything else at the festival. I know I'm allergic to peaches. I know I should have taken my EpiPen with me, but I wasn't planning on eating anything with peaches in it. It's not like it's a common ingredient in chili. I thought I was safe. Well, we all know how that turned out.

I'm sure I'll get an ear-full from Porter when I see him. And I can't even argue with him. I know better. I should have done better. I can't even argue that he's overreacting or being extra medical about it. I just hope Millie, Kiersten, and Amara never hear about it. The last thing I need is my overprotective mother hens to start lecturing me as well. You'd think I was the baby of the group rather than the oldest with how much they fuss over me.

I bolt up when I hear a rustling sound. I grab the alarm clock off of the side table ready to launch it at whatever is making that sound. I finally muster the courage to look, and I'm equal parts relieved and startled to see Porter curled up on the floor with what I can only presume is the bedspread from his room.

I have a sudden flood of memories of the Teletubbies theme song and what feels like a fever dream where I basically mauled Porter. Oh, please tell me that was a dream. Please, oh, please, tell me I didn't ask to see his TV. I sink back down into my cocoon of blankets trying, and failing, to hide from my shame. My phone starts buzzing on the night stand. I pick it up and see Millie's face staring back at me. I slip out of bed and move as quietly as possible and head to the bathroom.

"Hey, Mills."

"You had an allergic reaction?!"

"How did you hear about that?"

"Porter called last night, but that's beside the point. You ate peaches! You didn't have your EpiPen on you! How careless could you be, Torrance?"

I wince at the use of my full name. Millie hardly ever calls me Torrance. She's one of the few people who I allow to call me Tori.

"He called?"

"Yes. Last night. He was worried about you and wanted us to know. He called Carson too, so be ready for that phone call."

"He called last night, and this is the first time I'm hearing from you? I'm shocked."

And just like that I'm back to my usual sarcastic tone. No better way to hide how I'm really feeling. I appreciate Millie's concern, but I can't deal with any of this right now. I know I was irresponsible, and I messed up. I don't know what's worse, knowing that everything that happened was my own fault or that I had an audience to my failure.

"Well, you can thank my husband for that. I wanted to get into the car and keep going until I got to you."

"I'm fine."

"Just because you're okay doesn't mean I don't worry about you."

I slump down on the floor. We aren't just talking about last night. Sometimes I hate how well she knows me. I wish I could just dig deep into the walls that I have built and be invisible. I wish people only saw what I wanted them to see. Part of me knows that isn't true, but I don't want to deal with the rational part of my brain.

"You haven't been yourself in a long time, Tor. Something is going on that you aren't telling us about. That you aren't telling *me* about. And I get it, I don't live at the house anymore. Things have changed. But you aren't talking to Kiersten either. You're shutting us out. What is going on?"

"I don't know. I guess I'm just feeling restless. I feel like I'm being left behind. You're married. Amara's engaged. Kiersten is finishing up with school, and then she will be on to new things. Jonathan is living life with his dream job. Everyone is moving on, and I'm still right where I was when we all moved back to Ridgeview. I'm stuck, Mills."

"Then get unstuck."

I snort. "Oh, just that simple, huh?"

"I never said it was simple. I just mean that you need to figure out what you want and then work like heck to get it. I've never met anyone more determined than you to get what they want. That's how you not only double majored in college but graduated early. That's how you—"

"Alright. Alright. I get it. I'm stubborn."

Millie giggles, and I'm sure it has nothing to do with me. I hear a muffled, "Stop it. I'm on the phone."

I kind of gag, but I'm also happy for my best friend. I just don't want to hear it.

"I'm going to go. Tell Mark hi for me. And thank him for keeping you...*occupied* so you didn't get in a car and drive all night."

I hear another giggle. "Okay." Giggle. "Bye, Tor." Giggle. "Just...be safe, okay?"

"I will. "

Giggle.

I hang up the phone but stay on the floor. I'm lost in my thoughts when there's a faint knock on the door.

"Torrance?" Porter calls softly. "You okay in there?"

I lift myself off the floor and look in the mirror. I wipe away any trace of tears and splash some cool water on my face before I open the door.

"I'm fine."

He looks at me with concern. "You sure?"

"Yeah." I walk out the door trying not to make eye contact. "Sorry for last night. I should have been more careful."

"It's fine."

I turn to face him. "No, it's not. I was irresponsible, and I should have known better."

"Torrance—"

"No." I step away from his outstretched hand. I don't need him to comfort me. Millie was right. I'm determined and don't need anyone. "I apologize for any inconvenience, and it won't happen again."

"Okay." He pauses. "I guess I'll head back to my room and start getting ready to leave then."

"Sounds good." I swallow back the emotions as they threaten to break free again.

"Tor?"

I look up into his face laced with concern, and I don't know what comes over me. Before I can think it through, I'm closing the distance and pressing my mouth to his. He's tentative at first, but soon he wraps his arms around my waist and starts to take over. And for once, I let him. I'm lost in the moment. Lost in him.

I shift as I try to deepen the kiss even further. Our mouths are a frenzied tangle. A wordless fight for control. Porter tightens his grip on my hip as he moves me against the wall. He trails hot kisses along my jaw and down my neck and back up again until he finds the soft spot below my ear. I let out a soft gasp. I've kissed guys before. I've made out with a few, but I've never been kissed like this before. I've never kissed anyone like this before.

A surge of need for dominance takes over as I grab Porter's shirt and turn our tangled bodies until it's his back up against the wall. It's my turn to control, and Porter lets me.

We go back and forth, each taking our turns while the other is completely at their mercy. When we finally pull apart, I'm gasping for air. I don't even have to look in the mirror to know my hair is a complete tangle of wild curls, and my lips and face are chafed from the stubble that dusts Porter's jaw.

Porter's rumpled appearance tells me he's as disheveled as I feel. We each take a wall and just stare at each other as we each work to catch our breath.

"That was…"

"Yeah…it was."

"So what do we do now?"

Porter takes a tentative step forward. My heart races just at the sight of him. How was it just a week ago that I completely despised him? Now, well, now all I want to do is continue with what we were doing before biology told us we needed to breathe. Who really needs breath anyway? Breathing is overrated. I'd much rather make out with Porter.

A laugh bubbles out of me. Did I just giggle? Millie might be on to something.

"Did you just giggle?" Porter grins at me.

I can't fight the smile that breaks through. "I think I did."

Porter continues walking towards me slowly, and I'm powerless against his gaze. When he stops, I crave for him to close the distance the rest of the way, but when he runs a finger down my bare arm, there are goose bumps. He intertwines our fingers.

"I want to say something, but I don't want you to bite my head off."

I roll my eyes, but my smile widens at the same time. "I won't bite your head off."

His eyes crinkle at the corners as he smiles down at me. "Our history would prove otherwise."

I lean my head back on the wall trying to look serious, but the pure elation of whatever is going on makes it impossible to glower. "I won't bite your head off. Promise."

"Okay." Porter lets go of one of my hands and traces my jaw. I lift my hand to take his and keep it pressed against my cheek. The warmth gives me strength as much as it makes my heart skitter. Porter takes a deep breath as his eyes bore into mine. His eyes dilate as he takes me in, and it takes everything in me not to jump him again. "I want to do this right. I want to give this a chance."

"You do?"

"I'm pretty sure I've spent a majority of the time we've known each other being into you."

I giggle again. What is up with that? "You have? I seem to remember you not liking me when we first met."

His hand falls away from my face, and he steps away starting to pace the room. "You're unlike anyone I've ever met. I wasn't my best that night, and I shouldn't have gone to that party. I didn't exactly make the best impression."

"I never exactly gave you the opportunity to change my mind. I made up my mind what you were like, and that was that."

Porter sits on the bed. "What exactly did you think of me? I've never really known. I just knew you didn't like me."

I tentatively go and sit next to him. "That you were a stuck-up player."

He snorts. "A player? I mean, I can understand how you thought I was stuck up. I was so rude that night, but a player? Hardly."

"Well, every time I saw you you had a whole throng of girls hanging on your every word. Then when we had that class together, you had both of those girls all but fighting over your attention. I just figured you were like every jock I had ever known."

Porter takes my hand in his. "You might have been watching, but you weren't paying close attention. If you had, you would have noticed that all of that attention was one sided. I'm not like Trent. I don't like attention. I actually kind of hate it. I was so uncomfortable when that happened. It only got worse when people would find out that he was my cousin."

"What about all those dates Duncan would say you were on?"

"Duncan wouldn't leave me alone when I wanted to stay home and study. Or just not be around people. I figured out real quick that if I told him I was going on a date he would leave me alone. Anytime he asked about my dates, I told him I didn't kiss and tell."

Hearing how wrong I have been in my assumptions of Porter is like a sucker punch. I've been so misguided and pig-headed. I'm been so unfair.

"I'm so sorry I misjudged you." The words seem inadequate, but it's the best I have.

"Do you think if we would have met under different circumstances that things would have been different?"

I shrug. "I don't know. I was pretty self-involved back then. I probably still am."

Porter gives my hand a squeeze. "You're far from self-involved. You care too deeply for people to be self-involved."

"Do I, though? If that was the case, then why do I feel so conflicted about all of my friends moving on with their lives? Or why didn't I leave school to help my sister when she needed me most? Instead, she had to move to Valley Creek to live with Bonnie. I could have—"

"Could have what? You were what, twenty-two?

"I could have helped." My throat feels thick with emotions. I try to swallow them down, but my heart rate is increasing, and it's getting harder to breathe.

"Hey, eyes on me." Porter grabs my shoulders and makes me face him. "Deep breaths."

I shake my head. "I keep messing up." A sob escapes.

Porter pulls me into him, "You didn't mess up. You're human."

"That sounds a lot like an excuse."

"Not an excuse, just the truth. Just because you care deeply doesn't mean you have to be the one to take care of everyone. Trust me, I know. I'm guilty of the same thing. I have to be in charge; if I'm in charge, then I can control what happens. Somehow, I've convinced myself that that means I'm taking care of people."

I take a staggering breath. Porter just put into words everything that I have felt for years but never knew how to say. I don't like change, and I don't like feeling out of control. Like last night. I messed up, I got sick, I lost control, and bad things happened. I mean, I'm fine, but it could have been so much worse.

"Then there was you."

I start to pull away from him slightly, not fully sure I want to know where this is going to go.

Porter continues, "You were—well, are—unpredictable. I couldn't control how you made me feel. You just blew into my life and were this thorn that wouldn't go away. A conundrum I couldn't figure out."

"You make me sound delightful," I say dryly.

"You have your moments."

I smile at that.

"I was so focused on what I didn't understand that I did everything in my power to push away what I was really feeling."

I pull back more so that I can face him more fully. "And what was that?"

Porter doesn't get the chance to answer. His phone starts to ring, and when he looks down, concern laces his features.

"I'm sorry. I have to take this," he says as he gets up and answers the phone. "Zayna, what's wrong?"

I try to school my features. I won't let my jealousy get the best of me. Porter has been nothing but honest with me. I won't assume the worst. I believe what he said about not dating around. I'm choosing to believe that he wouldn't be talking to me like this if he was involved with someone else.

Porter steps into the hall, and I spend the entire time willing myself not to spiral into thoughts of who Zayna is and why she would be calling Porter so early in the morning. I've mostly been successful when Porter slips back into the room.

"Sorry about that."

"Is everything okay?"

"Yeah. Zayna was just letting me know that Suki got into my room and made a bit of a mess. Which is what I get for leaving her for so long."

I nod, not sure what to say.

Porter makes a point of catching my eye. "Tor, you have nothing to worry about. I meant what I said, you've been it for me for a long time. Even if I didn't admit it to myself, it's only been you for years. Suki is my dog. And Zayna is—"

He doesn't get to finish his explanation. I cut him off as I press my mouth to his.

This kiss is much less frenzied than the first, but it still makes my heart race just as much.

"It doesn't matter who Zayna is. I trust you."

Porter rests his forehead on mine. "Do you?"

"I want to," I admit. "I don't trust easily, but I'm pretty stubborn and usually get what I want."

"And what is it that you want?"

"You." My voice is quiet, but it's the truth. "I think I've been lying to myself just as much as you have. It's always been you. I just didn't realize it until I saw you sleeping on my floor this morning."

"It was worth it if it got us here."

"I mean, I could have done without the allergic reaction," I admit.

"Yeah, that was a little dramatic."

I shove him. "Shut up. It's not like I did it on purpose."

He laughs, and my heart melts a little at the sound. "I know you didn't. It was an accident, but promise me you'll keep your EpiPen on you."

I nod. "I promise."

He holds out his hand, pinky extended towards me. "Nope, I'm going to need more than just a promise."

CHAPTER 25

Porter

I T TOOK US longer to get on the road than it probably should have this morning, but you won't hear me complaining. Each and every kiss was worth the delay. Driving in the car with one hand on the steering wheel and one on Torrance's thigh as she traces intricate patterns up and down my arm is distracting in the best way. I would go through all the headaches of last night a thousand times if it meant we would end up here. Not that I want her going into anaphylactic shock. Okay, so maybe not the best example, but the sentiment is the same. Whatever has led us here, right to this moment, it has been worth it.

Tori and I had a long overdue heart-to-heart. I shared things with her that I haven't ever shared with anyone. Not even my family. It was hard to let her in like that, but for the first time in my life I wanted to. I wanted to let someone in enough to know the real me.

And then we kissed some more. Okay, a lot more. What can I say, we have a lot of time to make up for, and I am more than happy to make up for lost time.

An hour into our drive, Carson called. When she found out that we were on the road, she switched to FaceTime. One look at Tori's face and she screamed, "You've been kissed!"

Torrance tried to brush her off, but Carson wasn't buying it. I tried to hold back a laugh, but I couldn't. She smacked my arm, and I gave her thigh a squeeze, making her tanned skin tint with pink. And it was the prettiest shade I've ever seen.

Carson pressed and prodded as only a younger sibling can. Torrance finally had enough and faked a bad connection and ended the call. Carson clearly didn't buy it and immediately called back. She silenced her phone and went as far as throwing it into the back seat.

We spent the rest of the drive talking about everything and nothing. When we stopped for food and to fill the car with gas, I pulled her into an empty corner of the small convenience store and kissed her until we were both breathless. I'd be lying if I said I wasn't a little proud of the flush that crept up her neck as the store manager asked us to leave.

Not that she is all innocence. That little hurricane of trouble almost got us kicked out of the diner we went to eat at when she told them we needed a corner booth far away from prying eyes then proceeded to sit on my lap and whisper, "Now where were we?" before she started to nibble on my ear.

It took us moving to a table in the middle of the restaurant, sitting on opposite sides, before they would take our order. Even then we had eyes on us the entire time.

"You're going to pay for that," I warned.

Torrance beams with pride at her antics. "I look forward to it."

Oh, this woman! She might be the death of me. What a way to go.

"TAKE A LEFT."

"There isn't anything to the left. Everything in this town is right."

GPS stopped working about an hour ago. I don't know where we are or where we're going. We are literally in the middle of nowhere. We stopped a few miles back and picked up a map. Who knew you could still even buy paper maps? Evidently losing phone signal isn't too rare of an occurrence out here so they still have them. Torrance has taken it upon herself to use her very best navigation voice. If I wasn't so annoyed with the situation we find ourselves in, I would find it alluring. However, that is not currently the case, and I'm finding myself getting increasingly irritated at her.

"Will you just trust me? Take the next left. The booking information said it was a bit out of town. Left is out of town."

I growl, but I do as she says. Two more miles of nothing, and I'm about to turn around when a cluster of dwellings come into view. But something is off. The closer we get to the buildings the higher in the sky they seem to get.

"You booked us into a treehouse lodge?!"

Torrance just beams at me. "I mean, at first I just booked it to mess with you, but now that I'm seeing it up close and personal, it's turning out even better than I hoped."

"They're treehouses!"

"Yes, they are."

"They're fifteen feet up in the air!"

"Has anyone ever told you how smart you are?"

I glare at her. She just looks at me with all the innocence of the Cheshire Cat.

"Tor," I grit out.

"Porter."

"I don't do heights."

"Then I guess you're sleeping in the car tonight because this is where we are staying."

"I can always turn around and leave you here."

"You could, but we both know you won't. For one, you'd miss me too much. Two, it's getting late. And three, it's starting to rain."

I groan. She's right, and we both know it.

"Fine, but I'm not happy about it."

She pats my arm. "Relax. It's completely safe, and you're going to be fine. Look." I follow her hand to see what she's pointing at. "Each cabin has multiple ways up. You can take the rope ladder, or there is a set of stairs for the wimps."

With that, she's out of the car and dashing to the front office.

I take a few extra minutes to compose myself. I wasn't kidding when I said I don't like heights. I'm terrified. My grandfather once took me to the town fair, and we rode the Ferris wheel. We got stuck. I freaked out. It wasn't pretty. I all but peed my pants, I was so terrified. My stomach was churning. They had to call the fire department to get us out because I refused to climb down on my own. Though some might consider that self preservation and a willingness to live, my friends and family? Well, let's just say I haven't lived it down. Maybe if it had happened when I was ten and not eighteen it would be different, but somehow I don't think so. Instead, I'm the butt of all the jokes when it comes to height-related things. And you know what? I'm fine with that. They can laugh at me all they want as long as my feet are firmly on the ground.

When I walk into the lobby of the front office, I hear the tail end of what the receptionist is saying.

"I'm so sorry, Ms. Rodriguez, there seems to have been a slight mix up with your reservation. It seems that though you have booked one of our larger double-roomed clubhouses, we only have a single available."

"Oh." Torrance turns to look at me as I step beside her. "Are you okay with that?"

"I'm not okay with any of this," I mutter.

Torrance turns as the receptionist says, "I do have our honeymoon suite available if you'd rather that. It has a king-sized bed and the best view of the area. I can upgrade you at no cost and add two complimentary tickets to our on-sight restaurant since this was our mistake."

Torrance doesn't even hesitate to accept. "That would be wonderful. Thank you."

The receptionist eyes me, and I can feel her assessing gaze. I'm pretty sure I also see her doing a ring check on both me and Torrance. I step a little closer to Torrance just to make a point. She must see the same look that I do since she silently slips her hand into mine and gives my cheek a quick peck. Even with all of the kissing we have done today, that simple gesture still sends a jolt of lightning to my heart.

Or maybe it's the actual lightning outside.

"Looks like the storm is finally coming in," the receptionist says, peering through the glass door before getting back to work getting us all checked in. "Here are your keys and your dinner tickets. Tickets are good for dine-in or room service. If you lose power at any time, there are generators on the premises as well as flashlights and lanterns in the cabins. If you have any questions, don't hesitate to call."

Torrance takes the envelope containing everything and heads for the door.

I turn to the receptionist, seeing that she's still openly ogling me. "Um, is this place safe? I mean with the lightning and all?"

"We haven't had any issues or incidents in the twenty years we've been open." She smiles suggestively. "But if you get too worried, you're more than welcome to come and stay in my room."

"No need," Torrance breaks in. "He'll be just fine. Won't you, honey buns?"

Before I can respond, Torrance is pulling my arm, and I'm following her back to the car to get our things.

"Ow! You're going to pull my arm out of its socket."

She releases my arm. "Sorry."

My mouth quirks at the sight of her.

"What?" Her eyes narrow as she looks at me.

"Nothing…honey buns."

She rolls her eyes. "Okay. Let it out."

I release the laugh I was holding back. "You were jealous."

"I was not!"

"You so were!"

"I was not jealous. I was merely helping you get out of an awkward situation, but if you'd like to take her up on her offer, then be my guest." She sweeps her arm in the direction of the door.

"Not even a tempting option."

Torrance eyes me suspiciously. "Really?"

"I'm pretty sure we've established that you're the only one I want to spend time with." She visibly relaxes, and I can't help but press on. "I mean, read the room, lady. We *clearly* came in together. And we didn't argue about being upgraded to a honeymoon suite."

Torrance rolls her eyes. "You think you're pretty cute, don't you?"

"Not at all. *You* think I'm pretty cute. That is, if all the things you were whispering in my ear at the diner are to be believed. Personally, I think I'm ruggedly handsome." She glares at me. "Careful, don't want your face to get stuck like that. It would ruin the whole sexy boss lady aesthetic you've got going on."

IT TAKES ME twice as long to make it up the ramp to our cabin as it does for Torrance to climb the rope ladder contraption, but she doesn't mention it when I finally make it to our cabin completely soaked to the bone, because of course the flood gates opened up while I was carrying our luggage up.

In fact, Torrance has been pretty quiet since I called her sexy. Did I overstep? I meant it wholeheartedly; she is tantalizing. Her confidence and take-charge attitude is wildly attractive. It's part of what I always found so annoying about her, but now that I've openly admitted my attraction and feeling about her, yeah, it's sexy as heck.

I finally can't take it any longer. Torrance is out on the balcony watching the storm. I open the slider before I can chicken out.

"Did I do something wrong?"

She turns to face me. "No."

"Then why aren't you talking to me? I know things have moved really fast. I mean, just yesterday we were trying to keep the peace, and then today it's been all make-outs and acting like hormonal teenagers, but I thought…" I trail off, not really sure what I thought. I mean, sure the kissing was nice. More than nice, but that's not all that it's about. I genuinely like this woman.

"It is fast."

My heart sinks at her words. "Do you want to stop?"

"No! I mean, unless you do. You're right. We've been acting like teenagers sneaking around…" She trails off.

"I don't want to stop, I'm just trying to get a read on you. We were all banter and giving each other a hard time, then I told you I thought you were sexy and you shut down. I'm just trying to understand what happened."

Torrance shrugs. "I don't know. I guess I just don't know how to do this."

"To do what?"

"This!" She motions back and forth between us. "I've never really had a relationship."

That takes me aback; surely she's dated before. Not that I want to think of her with anyone else, but certainly I'm not the first.

"I mean, yes, I've gone on dates, and I've dated, but I tend to fall into situationships rather than relationships."

"Situationships?"

"You know, the will-they-or-won't-they. You spend all your time together, but there isn't any real commitment."

"Is that what you want?" It's not what I want, but I'm still trying to figure out what she's talking about.

"No... yes? I don't know!" Torrance starts to pace the balcony as she starts speaking so fast I can hardly catch any singular words. She slips in and out of English, going from French to Spanish and back to English. There might have even been a couple other languages I couldn't pinpoint in her rambling.

I finally take her by the shoulders and lead her back into the cabin sitting her on the couch.

"I'm sorry. I know I'm a mess."

"No need to apologize. Just talk it out. I might be able to give some insight to the situation."

"I don't need you to fix me, Porter."

I put my hands out in surrender. "I wasn't trying to fix you. I'm just saying, whether this is a situationship, as you called it, or leading to something more, I am the other half so I might have some insight. That is, unless you've already decided how this conversation is going to go. In that case, can you send me the transcript so I can have a clue as to what is going on?"

She sinks back into the sofa. "I'm sorry. You're right. I guess... I guess it's... it's just... I'm scared, Porter. I don't know what I'm doing. Not with this. Not with my life. I'm just flailing and failing over here. I feel like I'm drowning. Kissing you this morning was pure impulse."

I shift in my seat with unease.

"Not that I regret it! Because I don't. Not at all. In fact, it's one of the few things I don't regret lately." A little of the unease subsides, but Torrance isn't done so I sit and listen. "I hate my job, but I don't know why or what else I would do. All my friends are starting to pair off and get married, and I feel left behind. Then there's you." She looks at me. "I meant what I said earlier. You've captivated me for a long time, even if I wouldn't admit to it. I just don't know how to go forward. The last time I was this close to starting a relationship..."

I wait for a minute to see if she will continue before I finally speak. "What happened?"

Torrance gets a far off look in her eye as if she's going back in time.

"Oliver was always at our apartment since he was Kiersten's older brother. He was always around. I had an instant crush on him."

I clear my throat but don't say anything. I refuse to feel jealous over something that happened so long ago. Especially since I knew the object of my jealousy is no longer earthside. I remember when Kiersten's brother died back in college. I narrow my focus back to Torrance as she lets the words out.

"Nothing ever really happened. We'd hang out, especially during the summer when everyone else would go home between semesters. We both stayed. Me to work, him to train and practice. He was so determined to make it to the NHL. That last summer we flirted more than ever before. I went home for a few weeks before the next semester started, and Oliver never texted. I just figured he was busy with training. Only, when I got back to school, Oliver had a girlfriend. Then a few months later...well...You know what happened next. The semester ended. Kiersten and Oliver were driving back to Minnesota for the break, and—"

"They never made it," I finish. My voice is thick. I knew of Oliver, though I never met him. The night of the accident was one of the longest of my life, and it's not like I was close with Kiersten. Amara had come into our apartment bursting with tears. Duncan had jumped into action, and soon we were helping the girls load up in his car and driving the two hours to the hospital Kiersten and Oliver had been taken to. By the time we had arrived, Kiersten was in surgery, and Oliver was on a ventilator. Their parents were on their way. Oliver's prognosis wasn't good. In the end, Kiersten survived. Oliver didn't.

I clear my throat. "Tor, I'm so sorry."

She wipes the tears from her cheek. "It wasn't your fault. You weren't driving the car that hit them."

I take her trembling hands in mine and do the only thing I can think to do. I pull them to my lips and kiss her knuckles.

"I never got the chance to ask him what happened. I went from confused to angry. I had watched him date countless girls over that time. And maybe that was his way of letting me down easy. There's no way of knowing," Torrance takes in a deep breath and expels it slowly. "I've never told anyone about that. Not even Jonathan or Millie. I certainly never told Kiersten. Before the accident, she would have been so upset with him. She had always warned us away from him. After, well, I didn't want her to have any negative feelings towards him."

"Why tell me?"

"I just... I just need you to understand where I'm coming from. I don't know how to date. I don't know how to let my guard down. I want to let you in, I really do. I just don't know how."

I pull her into my arms and rub her back as she sinks into me. "You let me in by talking to me." I tighten my hold on her. "Can I tell you a secret?"

She nods.

"I'm scared too."

She lifts her head and looks up at me. "You are?"

I nod. "My parents weren't exactly the greatest example of what a healthy relationship looks like. My mom fell hard and fast for my dad. They got married, had me. Then he took off."

"Porter, I'm so sorry."

"That isn't even the worst part. My parents didn't divorce. She kept hoping that he would come back. And he did, at least long enough for my mom to get pregnant with Zion. He took off for good when she was two. That time he asked for a divorce. My mom was so sad, but I think part of her was relieved. She didn't have to wonder anymore. She knew it was over. So, you're not alone in not knowing how to do relationships. I've chosen time and time again to remain single. I've never wanted to hurt like my mom did, or worse, hurt someone else like my dad did."

"So what you're saying is that neither one of us knows how to have a relationship?"

"What I'm saying is, you're the first person who's made me want to try."

Her eyes fill again. I catch a tear with my thumb as it streaks down her cheek.

"I want to try too."

"Then that's what we'll do."

"Can you do me a favor?"

"Anything."

"Will you kiss me?"

I trace her jaw with my thumb. "Thought you'd never ask."

I close the gap, pressing my lips to hers. This kiss is different from the others we've shared today. There isn't an urgency. It isn't fueled by attraction or impulse. It's just the two of us. In this moment together. A promise of trying. A promise of hope. It's soft and tender and healing.

TORRANCE AND I spend the rest of the evening wrapped up in each other. Sometimes talking, sometimes just listening to the rain hit the window. We take time to order food and eat when it arrives, then we go right back to the couch to sit by the fire in the fireplace. Kind of ironic if you ask me, to have a fireplace in a treehouse, but what do I know? I guess since it is electric and not actually wood burning, it's okay?

As much as I want to kiss Torrance more, I refrain. I need her to know that this is more than physical for me. If we're really going to give this a go, then it needs to be done right. Which also means I will be sleeping on the couch tonight.

Torrance yawns, and her eyes keep fluttering close.

"Why don't you head to bed?" I suggest.

"I'm fine," she says as she snuggles into me.

I kiss the top of her head. "Clearly." I sit up, causing her to do the same. "Go get some sleep. It's been a long day."

"Okay, fine." She gets up and makes her way to the bathroom. "Give me fifteen minutes, then you can have the bathroom."

"I'm not in any rush."

Torrance closes that door and I pull out my phone to text my mom. She's been on my mind since I talked about my parents earlier.

> **PORTER:** Just checking in.

> **MOM:** All good. How is the road trip? Your sister said you stopped by to see her. I know it meant a lot to her.

> **PORTER:** It was good to see her. I had no idea she was that good.

> **MOM:** She's worked hard.

> **PORTER:** It shows.

PORTER: I was actually wondering how you would feel if we stopped by tomorrow.

MOM: I would love it! Are you sure you have time? I know you are on a strict schedule.

PORTER: We can make it work. We have a built-in buffer. And it's not like Amara's grandparents live that far from Grantsville. If we stayed the night, we'd only have about a four hour drive the next day. Plenty of time before everyone else starts showing up.

MOM: When you say "we" do you mean you and Torrance individually, or has my son finally seen the light?

PORTER: Funny you should mention that...

My phone starts dinging incessantly as Torrance comes out of the bathroom. I suck in a breath. She really is something to behold, even in mismatched pajamas and her curls fighting the braid she's trying to wrangle them into.

"What?" She asks when she catches me watching her.

"Nothing. Just thinking how amazing you are."

Her cheeks darken with a blush which only adds to her beauty.

My phone dings again.

"Everything alright?" Torrance asks.

"Yeah. It's just my mom." I stand up. "Actually I was thinking maybe we could stop by for a quick visit tomorrow since we'll be so close."

"Of course."

"Are you sure? We've already stopped to see my sister. I really didn't intend for you to meet my whole family in the span of three days."

"Porter, you met three fourths of my family on the first day and then proceeded to spend an entire weekend with them. I think I can handle one day. Besides, I kind of like you more than I did three days ago." She gives me a saucy grin as she walks towards me.

"Oh, do you now?"

"Mmhmm." She loops her arms around my neck and starts playing with the hair at the nape of my neck, sending sparks throughout my entire body.

"And what are you going to do about that?"

"This." She rises up and presses a kiss to my lips. I tighten my grip on her curves to deepen the kiss, then think better of it. I pull back. At the questioning look in her eyes, I kiss the tip of her nose.

"It's important to me that you know this isn't just physical for me."

"I do."

"And I also need you to know, if you keep kissing me like that, it's going to be hard for me to be a gentleman. Especially since we are sharing a room tonight. And for that reason, I'm sleeping on the couch. I don't want us to rush into anything we aren't ready for."

Torrance sighs. "It's probably best that one of us has a clear head, but did you have to have it right then? That kiss was just getting good."

I laugh. "Which is why I needed to end it."

"Fine." She fake pouts. "You sure you don't want to share the bed? I mean, it's huge. There's plenty of room. We can even put up the cliché pillow barrier like they do in the movies."

"Too tempting. I'll stay on the couch."

"At least let me sleep on the couch. You already slept on the floor last night."

"And risk my mother and grandmother finding out? No, ma'am."

"Did you just 'ma'am' me?"

"I did, and I will again if you don't get in that bed."

She finally gives in and gets into the bed with a sigh. Once she's all situated, I finally go into the bathroom to change into my joggers and t-shirt. When I come out, Torrance is asleep. I walk over to the light and turn it off and brush a kiss to her temple. She sighs and sinks deeper into the blankets.

"Goodnight, Tor."

"Goodnight, Po."

I smile at the nickname and make my way back over to the couch.

CHAPTER 26

Torrance

*I*T'S OFFICIAL. I love Porter's family. We arrived right before dinner, and Porter's grandmother and mom went all out making all of his favorite foods. The Porter I know is a major health nut, but evidently he hasn't always been that way. I couldn't help but smile when I saw the bowl of chicken and dumplings sitting next to sausage and biscuits. My smile only grew when I saw the glare on Porter's face as he looked over and saw my amusement. Look, I might like the man now, maybe even more, but I'm not going to stop messing with him. My motivation might just be a little different.

"Mrs. Gentry, this all looks amazing!"

Porter's grandmother smiles over at me. "Thank you, dear. And call me MarMar. Everyone else does."

"All because of Porter." His mother, Annie, says as she pats his arm. He smiles down at her, but there is no denying the tint of pink crawling up his neck.

"Okay, we can stop, now."

"No, we shouldn't," I laugh.

"Yes, we should," Porter grits out.

"Leave the boy alone," Mr. Gentry says as he enters the dining room, giving his wife a kiss on the cheek and his daughter a hug.

"Thank you! Grand—"

Porter stops as his grandfather continues, "We'd much rather hear about our guest." He turns to me. "We've heard so much about you over the years, and I can see why you've captivated my grandson's attention for so long."

I hear Porter groan beside me. If the heat radiating from my face is any match to Porter's face right now, I'm not the only one embarrassed. I know Porter has talked about me over the years, Zion mentioned it and he's admitted to it, but having the rest of his family bring it up just makes it that much more real.

We talked and visited over dinner. I shared more than I normally would have with people I just met. There is something about Porter's family that puts me at ease. I feel welcomed and accepted, making it much easier to share when I usually don't.

It didn't hurt that I also got to see all the embarrassing baby pictures. Not that they were that embarrassing. It's really unfair how adorable Porter was. Either he never went through an awkward stage, or...

Or I'm more into him than I thought I was.

OG Roommate Group Chat

MILLIE: On a scale of 1-100, how in love with Porter would you say you are?

KIERSTEN: They haven't even gone on an official date, Mills, give her a minute.

AMARA: I'm just going to take credit for this love match now.

MILLIE: As you should, but I get credit for setting them up on this road trip.

TORI: I knew it was a set up!

KIERSTEN: To be fair, I had nothing to do with it.

AMARA: Only because we knew you wouldn't be able to keep it quiet.

MILLIE: Yeah, sorry to break it to you, Kiersten, but you can't keep a secret if your life depended on it.

TORI: Like you're so great at it. Forget a bull, you were about as subtle as a bomb going off in a china shop.

MILLIE: I never claimed to be subtle. I just claimed I could keep it a secret that it was an ongoing plan.

TORI: Does this mean it was also a set up to have me be the one who had to go to his apartment to drop off the ring?

AMARA: I had nothing to do with that!

KIERSTEN: Neither did I.

TORI: That screams Amelia Jacobson.

MILLIE: It's Amelia Winters now, if you don't mind. And guilty.

TORI: I knew it!

MILLIE: I can't wait to rub it in Jonathan's and Mark's faces that I was right!

TORI: They were in on it, too? I mean, Jonathan sure, but I expected more from Mark. He's spent too much time with you.

MILLIE: I think what you mean is not enough time.

KIERSTEN: So does this mean I'm the last woman standing?

AMARA: You still have Trina!

KIERSTEN: Thank goodness for that!

MILLIE: Speaking of, I should add her to the group chat!

MILLIE: Okay added. Welcome to the group chat, Trina!!!

TRINA: What are we talking about?

AMARA: How we were all right and Tori and Porter love each other.

TORI: We don't love each other. It's been three days!

AMARA: I knew after three minutes that I was going to marry Duncan.

KIERSTEN: You haven't said "I do" yet.

TORI: Whoa, was that a snarky comment? Who took Kiersten's phone?

KIERSTEN: Ha ha ha. It's me. I'm just in a mood.

AMARA: You don't have moods.

KIERSTEN: You make me sound like a saint.

TORI: Because you are!

KIERSTEN: Hardly.

MILLIE: Care to share with the class what's going on?

KIERSTEN: Not really. This weekend is all about Amara. And this conversation is about Tori. I'll be fine.

TORI: I expect a full rundown of whatever is going on when everyone gets here tomorrow.

AMARA: No fair! I want in, too!

TORI: Fine, Sunday then.

TRINA: Has Duncan figured out that you know about this whole thing yet?

AMARA: Nope. He still thinks I think this is just an anniversary trip.

TRINA: Wouldn't you figure something was up if everyone was mysteriously out of town at the same time? Not to mention when you get on a plane to Tennessee?

TORI: Duncan isn't that complex.

MILLIE: Be nice.

TORI: I was!

AMARA: I think he's planning on telling me that we are going to visit my grandparents and that the party is the extra surprise? I don't know. Guess I'll find out.

MILLIE: It's really sweet how much he's trying.

AMARA: It is. Gosh, I love him.

TORI: Since 60% of this chat are in the same house, can we end this? Porter wants to show me the barn.

MILLIE: Awww, he wants to "show you the barn!" I'm so happy for you!!!

TORI: Will you get your mind out of the gutter? It's literally a barn. He grew up on a farm.

KIERSTEN: Like a real farm? Like with animals and everything?

TORI: Yep.

MILLIE: Don't let us stop you.

MILLIE: Just remember, hay will be a nightmare to get out of your hair.

TORI: Know I'm glaring at you through the screen.

MILLIE: Love you!

PORTER WASN'T KIDDING when he said he was going to show me the barn out back. This place is huge! Who knew it took so much to run a farm? Okay, so everyone probably knows that, but I'm a city girl. Give me a break. I grew up in an apartment. I didn't know how big an acre was until college. And I'm still not sure I really understand. If one more person tries to explain it in respect to a football field, I'm going to scream. News flash, I don't understand that either! Tell me in swimming pools or something. I grew up in California; I learned how to swim before I was three. Swimming pools, I understand.

"And that's about it," Porter says as he leads us to the end of the barn. I must have zoned out— or rather, I enjoyed seeing Porter in his element—and can't remember much of anything he said about the farm. I really don't care, but I love that he does. I get that he wanted out of this small town, but he still loves it.

"You really love this place, don't you?"

Porter shrugs. "It's home."

"Then why leave?"

"Because I don't want to be a farmer. This may be where I grew up and where my grandparents built their lives, but that doesn't mean I have to stay. I can always come home and visit. I much prefer city life. It suits me better."

"Could you ever imagine moving back to Tennessee?" I hate to ask, but if we're going to really try and make this thing between the two of us work, I need to know.

"I don't know. Maybe. I guess I never thought too much about where I'd end up. As much as I love order and planning, even I leave some things to chance."

"See, and I'm the opposite. I think more about where I'm going to end up and try to figure out a way to make it happen."

"Guess that's why we compliment each other." Porter wraps his arms around my waist and pulls me in close to him.

"Does it?" I ask. "I'm not trying to be a pessimist, I swear. I'm just trying to figure out how this will all work."

He tightens his arms around me. "It does. You add color to my black and white world." He nuzzles my neck, and I tilt my head, giving him better access. "And I hope I balance you out as well."

"You do." I straighten so I can look him directly in the eye. I need him to understand how much he helps me. "You ground me without making me feel like I'm flighty. You help me without trying to change me. You see me for me. There aren't a lot of people in my life who have done that. I've always been too much for people. Or not enough. With you, I feel like I'm exactly what I'm meant to be."

He clears his throat. "Just so we're clear, I'm going to kiss you now."

"Thought you never would."

For the record, I'm a big fan of barn kisses. Even when the cows start mooing and horses neigh.

I sigh as I lean closer into Porter. "You know, I've been thinking."

"About what?"

"That potatoes might just be exemplary vegetables." I squeal as Porter starts to tickle my sides.

"No one over the age of five can call me that."

"She's only four."

"Which means she has one more year."

"You planning on being around that long?"

"I'm planning on being around as long as you'll let me."

CHAPTER 27

Porter

I WAS NERVOUS TO bring Torrance here, not because I didn't want her to see Grantsville. And not because I didn't want her to meet my family. I was nervous because of how much I did want her here. I wanted to see her interact with my family. I wanted to see her laugh at MarMar's embarrassing stories from my childhood. I just wanted her here. In my home. The place where I can be nothing but myself. There are no pretenses here. Here, I'm just Porter. If she likes the man she sees here, then I know she really likes me.

"We should probably head back in," Tori says, and I'm reluctant to let her go.

"Do we have to?" I give a halfhearted protest.

She starts playing with the hair at my nape again, and it's driving me crazy.

"You know how you stopped everything last night in order to remain a gentleman and not push things faster than we're ready for?"

"Yes…?"

"Think of this as me remaining a gentlelady."

"That's not a word."

"Has anyone ever told you that you're annoying?"

"You. Repeatedly."

"At least you're aware then." She kisses me one more time then steps out of my arms. She grabs my hand and leads me out of the barn. "Come on. Your grandpa said something about musical charades, and I'm intrigued."

"You're going to annihilate us."

"Even better!"

IT WAS LATE when we finished Grandpa Gentry's version of musical charades, a game he made up when my mom and aunts were little. I'd explain, but the only consistent rule seems to be that there are no consistent rules.

After Torrance repeatedly beat the pants off the rest of us, even with Grandpa cheating and changing the rules midway through, we decided to call it a night. I helped Torrance carry her things to my sister's room, not because she needed the help, but because I wanted one more goodnight kiss. One without all the prying eyes. It was short-lived. MarMar and my mom showed up and shooed me to the guest room. I'm not even permitted to sleep in my own room since it's "just across the hall" from Zion's room.

"She's good for you," Mom says as I follow her and MarMar back downstairs to the living room.

"I like to think so," I say, smiling over at my mom.

"All it took was you finally admitting you had feelings for her," MarMar jokes.

"Actually, all it took was her going into anaphylaxis, but semantics," I joke.

"It's just so good to see you smile!" Mom gushes. "It's been too long. You're too serious these days."

"Agreed! Much too serious now!" MarMar shouts.

"Will you two leave the boy alone?"

"Thank you, Grandpa! Finally someone is on my side."

"Besides, anyone would smile if a girl like that thinks you hung the moon."

"Okay! That's enough." I stand up. "Now if you will excuse me, I'm going to go sleep in exile."

"It was for your own good! You're not stealing that girl's virtue under my roof!"

I stop in my tracks at my grandmother's words. "Steal her what? Who talks like that? Also, what kind of man do you think I am?"

"A good one, who's been in love with that girl up there for the better part of the last decade," Mom says. "All your grandmother was saying is that it's important to take your time."

"We are! We're still figuring things out. We haven't even gone on a date. And no one said anything about love."

All three share a glance.

"If you will excuse me, it's been a long couple of days and I'd really like to sleep in an actual bed tonight."

TORRANCE: That was some conversation you were having downstairs.

PORTER: How much did you hear?

TORRANCE: This house isn't as big as you think it is. And the walls are pretty thin.

PORTER: Great.

TORRANCE: I think it's sweet. I wish my parents cared half as much about what I did as your mom and grandparents do.

PORTER: You don't talk much about your parents.

TORRANCE: Not much to tell. They still live in Ridgeview. I see them once a week, and they still would rather work than do pretty much anything else. At least I have Carson and Bonnie. Speaking of which, Carson called again.

PORTER: And what did she have to say?

TORRANCE: Well, Aly was talking about a potato. It was all super random.

PORTER: Sounds it.

TORRANCE: You wouldn't know anything about that, would you, Po?

PORTER: She's four. It could be anything.

TORRANCE: It's getting late. We should probably get some sleep.

PORTER: You're probably right.
Goodnight, Tor.

TORRANCE: Goodnight, Po.

CHAPTER 28

Torrance

AFTER WHAT MIGHT possibly have been the best sleep of my life, Porter and I ate breakfast with his family before heading out. Today's drive is so much shorter than the previous days, but I'm having mixed feelings about this trip ending. On the one hand, I'm so ready to sleep in my own bed and not be trapped in the car all day. On the other hand, I'm scared that once we're not in our protective bubble, things with Porter will go sideways. I know that isn't fair and that we've talked a lot about the past and our hopes for the future, but it doesn't stop the doubts from creeping in. I'm the queen of situationships, and a dunce when it comes to relationships. I have no idea how to even have one. My one and only real boyfriend was in high school, and it lasted maybe three months. That might be a long time in high school, but it's not in the grand scheme of things.

I can't tell what Porter is feeling. Is he feeling torn on what could happen too, or is he just picking up on my feelings? Either way he hasn't said anything, which, again, mixed feelings. It's possible he just doesn't want to ruffle feathers, but since he's had no problem calling me on my crap up to this point...

"Are you okay?" I jump at the sound of Porter's voice.

"Fine."

He reaches over and takes my hand in his. "How about you tell the truth?"

Uggh! Why am I so aggravated with him? Isn't this exactly what I wanted him to do? To notice how I was feeling and bring it up? So now that he is, why do I have to go back to my old reliable sarcastic tone? I take a deep breath and try to calm my nerves. This needs to be brought up, and as much as I would rather live in this little bubble we've created, that isn't realistic.

"Not really."

"I could guess, but I know you'll just get mad at me for putting words in your mouth." He turns to look at me. "Even if I'm right."

I glare at him, but my heart isn't in it. "You think you know me so well."

"Am I wrong?"

"No," I answer reluctantly.

A smile plays at the corner of his mouth. One that I would rather kiss than have this conversation.

"I guess I'm just scared about what's going to happen next."

"I think I've made my intentions pretty clear. I want us to go on a date. I want us to give this thing between us a real shot."

I shift in my seat. "I want that too. I'm just scared that once this little bubble we've been in pops..."

"That what? I'll change my mind? I don't know about you, but I don't usually bring my family into situations where I feel casual."

He's right. I know he's right. I've literally met his entire family this week. And he's met most of mine. He's known my friends as long as he's known me. He knows everyone whose opinion matters most to me.

I swallow hard. "So what do we do?"

"We finish the last thirty minutes of this drive. We unload all this junk out of the car. Then we're going to change because I'm taking you on a date. Even if that date is just a walk around the O'Malley property, because I love you, but if I have to get back in the car before Monday morning, I might cry."

Porter's phone rings before I can process everything he just said.

I HEAR MILLIE before I see her. Porter pulls up the gravel road to Amara's grandparents house, and I see a vibrant ball of color jumping up and down, squealing with delight.

"Surprise!" She yells as I'm swept into a big hug the moment I open the car door. "Bet you didn't expect to see us early!"

"I didn't, but I should have known better." I smile at my best friend. If there is one thing Millie is, it's a party-throwing machine, just like her mother. I'm happy to have her here. I could use some perspective. I'm still trying to process all that was said in the car during the drive. Even before the moment when I'm pretty sure Porter told me he loved me. That alone has the potential to make me go insane as I overthink and overanalyze all the possible implications.

Millie releases me from the hug, and I'm immediately wrapped into another one by Jonathan.

"I didn't even see you there," I joked.

"How could you? Hurricane Millie kind of took over," he laughs.

I hug him again. Millie might be the life of the party and the one who livens me up, but Jonathan gets me. He gives perspective without trying to fix things. Which is great because I could use a lot of that right now. I'm instantly less anxious knowing he's here.

"Heard that!" Millie yells.

"Wasn't trying to hide it," Jonathan counters.

I notice movement out of the corner of my eye and see Mark, helping Porter unload all the things.

"Hi, Mark."

"Torrance," Mark nods.

The next hour is a bit of a whirlwind which is to be expected when Millie is around. Especially when she's excited. She's never been to Tennessee before, and she's determined to see as much as she can before she leaves. Which is how we find ourselves back in the car yet again as we head back to the center of Nashville.

I lean over to whisper in Porter's ear, "You didn't have to come. I know you were tired and didn't want to get back in the car."

He shrugs. "What I wanted was to spend time with you, so what does it matter if it's here or there?"

I smile as I sit back in my seat, catching Jonathan's smirk from my other side. Because yep, you guessed it, I lost the seat battle and have the middle seat. Though it's not too bad in this instance.

"Better be careful. If Millie catches you two looking at each other like that, she's going to be planning your wedding next."

I roll my eyes. "Good thing she and Mark are still obsessed with each other then."

"Don't remind me," he groans.

I snort. "How was traveling with them?"

"As awkward as you'd think it would be."

My cackle gets everyone's attention. I cover my mouth, but it's too late. Millie is zeroing in on me.

"What's so funny back there?"

I'm not one to shy away from the blunt truth so I tell her, *mostly.* "Just hearing about how awkward it was traveling with the newlyweds."

"We weren't that bad!" Millie protests.

"We kind of were," Mark mutters under his breath, but we still hear him.

Millie smacks him in the arm, and he starts tickling her with one hand while the other stays on the steering wheel. Millie squeals.

Porter leans across me to look at Jonathan, "If they were anything like this, you have my deepest condolences."

The whole car erupts into laughter, and the awkward tension lifts. Everyone is enjoying the ride and a night out until we see where Millie has dragged us all too.

THERE'S A COLLECTIVE "No!" as we stand outside the karaoke bar.

"Why?" Millie asks innocently. Or as innocently as she can while wearing a devilish grin.

"We're not singing," I say for the group.

"Why not?" Millie argues. "Don't act like you can't sing." She points at me and Jonathan accusingly.

"Never said we couldn't," Jonathan replies.

"Mills, half the fun of going to karaoke is to sing when you can't sing. People don't want to hear us. It will seem like we are showing off."

Mark tries to stifle a laugh.

"You're not helping," Millie gives her husband a sideways glance.

"Sorry." He doesn't look sorry at all, but to his credit, he schools his features enough to appease Millie.

Porter clears his throat. "Not to get involved in all this, but we're kind of blocking the entrance. We could always go to an open mic night. There's bound to be several of those around. I think I saw a sign for one a couple blocks back."

"Great idea!" Jonathan cheers. "I vote we do that."

"Me too!"

"But—"

"You wanted to see downtown Nashville. This is downtown Nashville," I say cutting her off. "We can do karaoke anytime. Seeing the next possible country star before their big break? Now that's not something we can do back home."

"Fine," Millie relents. "But you two owe me a karaoke night when we get back."

"Absolutely!" Jonathan and I sing in unison. Then we laugh. It's something we've done since we were kids, but for whatever reason it's still hilarious when we do it.

"We can take you to Treble Tone," Jonathan says.

I do everything in my power to school my features when all I want to do is kick him in the shin. He knows that's my special space. The space no one, other than he, knows about. And the only reason he knows about it is because he's the one who took me there the first time.

Jonathan turns and looks at me like a cat who caught the canary.

I glare.

He throws an arm around my shoulder, "What's wrong, Tor?"

His eyes dance with mischief until I elbow him in the stomach, and he doubles over. I don't even look back to see if he's hurt or laughing as I follow after Millie and Mark towards a café advertising an open mic night.

CHAPTER 29

Porter

AS MUCH AS I didn't want to go out tonight, I have to admit it was fun. After the whole karaoke debacle, we found a little café right down the street that was having an open mic night. They had some great talent. Millie wanted to go dancing but was eventually persuaded to head back to the O'Malley's house after Torrance began yawning. I'm still not convinced it wasn't an act since once we got back in the car, she was wide awake. Not that I'm complaining. I was more than ready to head back and definitely didn't mind her threading our fingers together and laying on my shoulder the whole drive back.

Mark parks the car, and everyone starts filing out of the car. Torrance releases my hand and does a big stretch and yawn.

"It's been a long day. I'm ready for bed." Okay, so maybe she wasn't pretending earlier. I get it, we have had a long day. I was just kind of hoping we would get some alone time once we got back, but that can wait until tomorrow. Or even when we get back. I meant what I told her. I'm not going anywhere until she tells me to.

"Okay," Millie says, then looks over at Mark. "We're probably going to head that way soon too."

"Gross!" Jonathan groans.

Millie just rolls her eyes. "Will you get over it? You know we're married."

"Yeah, but he's still my brother, and it's gross."

Mark claps Jonathan on the shoulder. "Goodnight, little brother."

By the way both Millie and Torrance laugh, I'm sure there is more to all of that than I understand. I can't even imagine what it would be like to have your best friend married to your sibling. Thankfully I won't ever have to find out. Zion and I don't live near each other, nor do we run in any of the same circles. A major pro for the eight-year age gap between us. Besides, Duncan is my only close friend who isn't related to me, and he's engaged.

As we all make our way up the stairs, Jonathan turns towards me, "Looks like they have us bunking together."

I look to where Amara's Oma has printed out each of our names and placed them on the corresponding door to where we will be staying. It's sweet how much time and energy both she and Papa O have put into this. Duncan did a good thing having this party here. It really does mean so much to them to be a part of this for their granddaughter.

"Looks like it."

We open the door to where our luggage is waiting for us. I head towards my bed and start to pull out my clothes to change for the night.

"You might want to wait before changing."

I look over at Jonathan. "Why?"

"Because I give Torrance about five minutes before she's knocking on the door asking you to go on a walk with her."

I raise an eyebrow.

"You didn't really think she was tired, did you?" He laughs. "She was just trying to get away from Millie."

"Aren't all of you friends?"

"The very best of friends." He laughs again. "That's why I know you have about four minutes until Torrance shows up at the door. Tori is very private about her feelings where Millie isn't."

"Didn't she and your brother hide their relationship from you?"

"I mean, technically, but if I would have been a better friend, I would have seen what was going on."

"Duncan said you and Mark had a full-on fist fight on the lawn."

"Not my finest moment, but more to my point, Millie loves anyone and everyone, and she shows it. Tori, on the other hand, is more selective. Once she selects you, you're in. Forever."

Something in the way he says forever makes me look him in the eye. There's a challenge. A warning.

"Is this where you ask me what my intentions are?"

"Not in so many words."

I smile. "You're a good friend, Jonathan."

"And you're not answering my question."

"You didn't actually ask it, but I have every intention of being around."

"Good!" Jonathan claps me on the shoulder. "And now, I do believe you are getting a phone call."

I look over at my bed where my phone is glowing, reading Torrance's name.

I arced my eyebrow at him.

"So I got how she was going to contact you wrong," he shrugs.

"Semantics?" I ask.

"Exactly! See, you get me."

I shake my head and laugh as I pick up my phone to answer it.

"I thought you were tired?"

"What gave you that idea?"

"The fact that you said you were tired."

"Oh, you poor thing. I assumed at least Jonathan knew what I was doing."

"He did."

"Did he give you the third degree yet?" I hear the amusement in her voice.

"Yep."

"Did you pass?"

"Yes!" Jonathan yells from his perch in the doorway between the bedroom and the en suite.

Torrance laughs. "Go look out your window."

"Why?" I ask as I do what I'm told. I look out the window and see Torrance next to what looks like an inflatable pool filled with pillows and blankets. She waves when she sees me.

"Come down."

I look over at Jonathan as he taps me on the shoulder holding out my jacket.

He shrugs. "I might have overheard some details before we went into town."

CHAPTER 30

Torrance

A SHIVER RUNS THROUGH me as I wait for Porter to come down. I don't know if it's because of nerves or because I'm cold. This idea seemed genius when I first thought it up, but now I'm second-guessing everything. I mean, I know Porter wanted to go on an actual date tonight, but then we ended up going out with everyone else. If I'm honest, spending the evening with Porter, alone, is what I wanted too. Which is how I came up with the idea of stargazing in the first place. Okay, so technically it was Papa O's idea. While we were all busy unloading the car and starting to unpack the boxes for the party, I asked him and Oma if there were any trails that would be good for a night walk. He mentioned how beautiful the sky is this time of year, and the rest is history. Or, I guess, present. Since you know, it's happening now. Okay, I really am nervous. I'm debating with myself about timestamps and proper terms.

It feels like it's taking Porter forever to get down here, though I know it's probably only a couple of minutes. I distinctly chose a spot that was on the opposite side of the house from where Millie and Mark are staying. I don't need any more prying eyes than necessary. Jonathan joked that he was going to watch Porter's every move when we were together, but I know he won't.

I finally hear the back door open and close, and I see Porter walking towards me with a tentative smile.

"What's all this?" he asks when he is about ten feet away.

"I thought we could learn how to sail," I deadpan. "What does it look like?"

Porter smiles, and it makes the butterflies in my stomach do a synchronized diving routine Tom Daly would be proud of. We're talking gold medal level precision.

My mind is racing, but that all stills when Porter takes my hand in his and threads our fingers.

"How do you do that?" I ask, staring up at him in amazement.

"Do what?"

"Calm my racing mind just by holding my hand."

"I don't know. You seem to have the opposite effect on me." He lifts our interlocked hands to his chest, letting go of my hand as he presses it over his heart. Even through the flannel and all the taut muscles that I never could quite learn the name of, I can feel the frantic pulse of his heartbeat.

I look up to see him studying me. Our eyes lock. I don't know if I pull him down or if he lifts me up, but we're in a frenzied entanglement of lips and teeth as Porter nips my lower lip, coaxing my mouth open to begin a thorough exploration and deepen the kiss. I have a faint awareness of us moving backwards as Porter tries to blindly find the fence post that is somewhere behind us, but in the process, the heel of my boot catches one of the blankets in the inflatable pool,and I go down, taking Porter with me.

We land with a thud, the pillows and blankets barely breaking the fall as I land flat on my back with Porter directly on top of me.

"Ow," I groan.

Porter moves his hands up and down searching for injuries.

"Are you okay?" He grabs my head and starts looking in my eyes.

I grab his hands to still them. His eyes look almost black in the dark, but I see the concern laced within them. "I'm fine. The blankets and pillows took the brunt of it."

Porter must realize that he's still practically laying on top of me and starts to shift. I move just enough that I can run both my hands up his torso and over his broad shoulders. If the look of desire in his eyes is any reflection of what I'm feeling, it's a good thing we're outside and I'm freezing.

Porter must feel it too, and just like in the treehouse, he has much better control than I do since he moves just enough to break the tension but not enough to break us fully apart.

After trying to use one hand to arrange the pillows and blankets, he finally gives up and reluctantly lets go of me to have use of both hands. Once he's done, he pulls me back into him. I settle into the crook of his arm with my head on his chest, listening to his steady heartbeat as he plays absentmindedly with my fingers splayed across his stomach. We sit there in relative silence, just watching the sky. When I start to shiver, he pulls me in closer as he grabs a blanket and wraps me up. Porter will occasionally point out different constellations and the mythology behind them. Both Greek and Norse. He really is such a nerd.

It's perfect.

CHAPTER 31

Porter

𝓘 WAKE UP WITH the sun in my eyes. I try to shield it with my arm, but it still takes me a moment to register where I am. Torrance shifts beside me, her unruly curls splayed across her face and pillow. I can't help but smile. Last night was perfect. Falling asleep outside wasn't exactly ideal, and sleeping in my contacts will have its consequences, but I wouldn't change a thing if it meant I woke up with Torrance in my arms.

The sun is still low in the sky, but I know I need to wake her. I don't know how early her friends wake up, but I have a feeling Torrance doesn't want it broadcasted that we spent the whole night together. I, on the other hand, wouldn't mind. It would save me from the Spanish Inquisition I know is coming my way. Let them all know once and for all that I'm completely smitten with their friend because I am completely and fully enthralled by her.

I roll on to my side to better face Torrance. She's so peaceful when she sleeps. I hate to wake her up.

"Tor," I say gently as I trace her cheekbone with my finger, "it's time to wake up."

She groans burrowing deeper into her cocoon of blankets. I laugh and try again.

"Torrance, you need to get up."

She swats my hand away.

"I don't want to." Her voice is muffled.

"I know, baby, but we need to get inside before everyone wakes up and notices we've been out all night."

That does it. She shoots straight up, her hair going every which way. It takes her a minute to acclimate to where we are.

"We fell asleep!" she says as if she's just putting two and two together.

I try to fight back my smile, but it's no use.

"We did."

Torrance turns to face me, and her face goes sheepish. "Did I do anything weird in my sleep?"

"You mean other than declaring your undying love of Tinky Winky?"

She shoves me in the arm. "Shut up."

We both laugh.

"Besides, I think we both know my favorite Teletubby is Po." She juts out her chin in mock retort as she looks up into my eyes.

I lean down, closing the gap. "I think we both know Po returns the sentiment."

Just as quickly as the kiss starts, Torrance ends it.

"Sorry. Morning breath," she says as she covers her mouth.

"I don't mind." I give her a wry smile, but she's right to end things. We need to get all of this cleaned up and go back into the house.

Once we get moving, it doesn't take long to get the pool deflated, the blankets folded, and pillows stacked where they go in the garage. Apparently stargazing is a big pastime, or at least it used to be, for the O'Malley family. Somehow I just don't see Amara's mom as someone who takes time to look at the stars anymore.

When we walk through the back door, there is movement in the house, but the only one to see us walk in is Jonathan.

"Morning," he grins as he lifts his coffee mug to his mouth.

I bite back a smile. "Morning, Jonathan."

"So…how was your night?"

Torrance shoves him in the arm. "Shut up."

I hold back a snort.

Millie comes through the door in full-on party planning mode with Mark shortly behind her.

"Hey, guys!" Millie says brightly. "Porter, are you an early riser like Tori is?"

Jonathan starts coughing as he tries to contain his laugh with a mouth full of hot liquid.

Out of the corner of my eye, I see Torrance elbowing him.

"Something like that."

Her eyes dart between the three of us. "What am I missing?"

"Nothing," Torrance and Jonathan say in unison. If she didn't buy it before, she certainly isn't going to now.

"So," I say interrupting whatever she was going to say, "what's the plan for today? Duncan and Amara get in around, what, six?"

Millie still looks between the three of us but answers me with a sigh of resignation. "Yes. And Kiersten and Trina should be here around noon."

Torrance uses the counter behind her to push off into the middle of the room. "Great, so until then we can all just relax."

She starts to head for the door.

Millie catches her arm. "Oh, no, you don't." The two of them look at each other and I'm pretty sure have a full conversation with nothing more than eye movements. "I need you to help unpack the centerpieces and start setting up the decorations." She then turns to the men in the room. "And I need the three of you to start setting up the tables and dance floor and build the stage for the band."

My eyes go wide. We're building a stage? I realize I don't have a clue what all has been planned for this party, but how are we supposed to get all of that done today before 6:00?

I must be the only one who doesn't think it's possible because both Jonathan and Mark hop to attention. Jonathan gives Millie a salute which makes Millie roll her eyes, and Mark gives his wife a quick kiss on the cheek as he follows his brother towards the door.

I look at Torrance, who gives me a shrug and a small smile then follows Millie deeper into the house.

I follow Jonathan and Mark and find them out back next to stacks of what looks like 2x4s. When Millie said we were building a stage, she meant it. Jonathan and Mark must see my bewilderment.

"Don't worry, it won't take too long," Mark says. "We've built a few of these over the years for Millie's mom. Usually takes about an hour. We aren't doing anything too fancy."

I'm still flabbergasted that this is what we are doing, but I get to work helping both of them move the planks of wood together and hold them while Mark uses the nail gun. Just as promised, we are done quickly and move on to our next task.

When we're done, the backyard actually looks like it's ready for an engagement party.

CHAPTER 32

Torrance

I FOLLOW MILLIE UPSTAIRS until we reach the room I will be sharing with the rest of the girls when they get here. When we enter, Millie closes the door behind her, and I don't like the gleam in her eye as she looks at the bed I didn't sleep in last night.

"Okay, now spill!" Next thing I know my best friend is pulling me down next to her on the bed as she sits cross-legged, eager for me to spill all the details.

"There's nothing to spill."

"First of all, lies. Second of all, I have eyes. Third of all, lies!"

I fall back on the bed, and for the second time in twelve hours, pillows break my fall. Okay, so this is nothing at all like the first time, but still. I grab a pillow and cover my face with a groan. Maybe if I pretend to be asphyxiated she'll leave me alone.

Millie takes the pillow and tosses it off to the side. "Pretending to be dead won't stop me."

She knows me too well.

I sit up, leaning on my elbows. "I have no idea what I'm doing, Mills. It's like one minute we're fighting over when to fill up the gas tank and the next we're making out until I'm completely breathless."

I roll over to my stomach burying my head in the comforter with a groan.

"Well, I'd tell you to stop overthinking things, but I'm clearly too late to that party."

I lift my head and look at her. "You're not helping. You're supposed to be helping."

"Well, Tor, we're in uncharted territory here. You've never liked anyone enough to get you to this point."

"Ugh, love is dumb!" I sit up. "Did I just say that?"

If the look of shock on Millie's face says anything, then I did, in fact, say that.

"I have no idea where that came from," I say, mid-panic.

"If I had to wager a guess, I'd say it came from your heart."

I fall back on the bed. "Hearts are stupid."

Millie laughs. "Yeah. Sometimes they are."

I look at Millie assessingly. "Why are you being so calm about all of this? I would have thought you'd be throwing a full-on parade."

"Oh, I am. It's a full-on electrical parade even Walt would be proud of in here," she says, tapping the side of her head.

I pick up one of the pillows and smack her with it. We both fall into a fit of laughter.

I still have no idea what's going on, but at least I feel lighter about it after talking with Millie.

EVERYTHING THIS MORNING and afternoon went off as smoothly as it could have, which is to be expected. Millie is nothing if not an excellent planner. Kiersten and Trina arrived and got straight to work putting centerpieces on the tables and putting together all of the floral arrangements. I'll be perfectly honest, I have no idea what all we brought with us from California. My job was more of a facilitator than anything regarding actual planning. I did, however, get the band for the evening.

By the time Duncan and Amara arrived, we had everything ready to go. All that was left was for Amara to hug her grandparents and for all of us to head to our rooms to get ready for the party.

"I have no idea what I'm wearing tonight," Trina complains as she looks through the myriad of options she pulled from her suitcase.

"How many did you bring?" Amara laughs.

"Seven. I didn't know how fancy everyone was going and wanted to be prepared."

"You could have just asked," Kiersten giggles.

"I *could have*, but what's the fun in that?" Trina winks. "Do we know who's on the guest list?"

"You mean, are there any cute guys coming?"

"Exactly! See, you get me!"

I laugh as I watch the exchange. I might have had a hard time with the change when Trina first moved into the house, but she really does fit in with us. They continue going back and forth as they finalize their outfits.

Kiersten comes behind me and wraps me in a hug. "You're quiet."

I look at her through the mirror. "A lot on my mind."

"It's okay to be happy, you know."

I nod.

"You're nodding, but I don't think you actually believe it." Kiersten releases me to turn me towards her. "Just because my brother was an idiot who didn't know what he missed out on doesn't mean you never put yourself out there again."

My breath stutters. "You knew about that?"

"I had a feeling something was going on. You were always together that summer, but when school started, he was dating someone else, and you wouldn't make eye contact with him."

"Are you mad at me for never telling you?"

"At first it hurt that you felt like you couldn't, but then I figured you'd talk to me when you were ready."

"I was going to. I just—I didn't know how to, especially after—"

Kiersten wipes a tear from the corner of her eye as she nods. "I know. And I appreciate that you were looking out for me."

I blink back my own tears.

"I told Porter about it. About Oliver."

"You must really trust him."

"I think so...maybe..."

Kiersten starts to say more when Millie bursts through the door.

"Who's ready to party?"

Everyone heads out the door to head downstairs to start greeting guests as they arrive. I hurry and finish getting dressed, then head down. I shake my hands and stretch my neck to relieve some of the tension as I walk down to the party.

I take one more deep breath before I open the back door, where the only question that matters is if Duncan actually pulled off throwing this party or not.

AUNTS, UNCLES, COUSINS, Duncan's parents, friends from college we haven't seen in years. They all came to celebrate Duncan and Amara. Well, everyone except her parents, but I guess none of us are too surprised they didn't show up. I just wish they would have come for Amara. I know how much she wanted them to be here.

A pair of strong arms wrap around my waist, and I lean back into Porter.

"We actually pulled it off," he says in my ear.

I nod. "We did."

He takes my hand and turns me to face him. "May I be so bold as to say how beautiful you look tonight?"

I blush under his gaze. I break eye contact and stare down at my dress. I suddenly feel very exposed standing here with him.

"Hey," Porter uses his finger to lift my chin to look up at him. "What's going on in that head of yours?"

"That I don't know what we're doing here." No use in lying. I've never been any good at it anyway, might as well be completely honest.

"I'm assuming you mean between you and me, and not the party."

"It's all just moving so fast, Porter."

"Is it really that fast though? I mean, we've known each other for years."

"Yeah, and up until four days ago, we didn't get along."

Porter grabs my hand and leads me to the side of the house where the guests aren't congregating.

"What's all this about, Torrance? I thought we talked about this."

"Did we really, though? I mean, we've hardly talked about what going forward really means. You've said you're not going anywhere, and I believe you. I don't want you thinking that I don't. But we've been in this little bubble. What happens now that we're back to our real lives?"

"I don't know. It's not like I have all the answers here. All of this took me as much by surprise as it did you."

"So what do we do?"

"We date."

"Just like that?"

"We never know unless we try, right?"

I know he's right. Or at least I want to. I'm just so much in my head. And my conversation with Kiersten didn't exactly help. I think I trust him, but I don't know. All the pieces of what I thought I knew and what was real have gotten jumbled in my head. I know I like him. A lot. I'm scared to be wrong, but I'm even more scared to be right. I trusted Oliver, and when that went sideways, it all but destroyed me. If how I feel about Porter is any indication, he has the power to completely demolish me.

"I—"

Jonathan comes around the corner before I can answer, not that I'm fully aware of how I would have even answered Porter. Do I want to make things work? I think so, but I'm also scared. What if I can't do it? What if even after everything we've shared and talked about I shut down and can't let him in?

"Tor, they need you in the house."

"What's going on?"

Jonathan rubs the back of his neck, a tell he's had since we were kids.

"Jon, what aren't you telling us?"

"Amara's parents showed up."

"Isn't that a good thing?" Porter asks.

"Not when Duncan didn't invite them, and Amara is inside in tears."

I look at Porter one more time. "I need to go."

I barely see his nod as I run after Jonathan towards the house. The whole way I swear under my breath. What was Duncan thinking? How could he be so dumb? He knows how important Amara's family is to her. Even if they chose not to show up, that would have been on them. This is on him.

CHAPTER 33

Porter

"T ELL ME AGAIN why you thought it would be a good idea to not invite her parents?"

It's been an hour since Jonathan came and got Torrance. To say Duncan made a mess of things is a gross understatement. Turns out my idiot best friend thought it would be a great idea to plan and host a surprise engagement at his fiancé's grandparents' home then invite all of their friends and family *except* her parents.

"Everything would have been fine if they hadn't shown up," Duncan complains as he splays out on my bed. The girls have been held up in their room since Amara's tearful exit from the party after the run-in with her parents. From the sounds of it, I'm glad I missed it. If nothing else, it gives me a slightly larger chance of summoning up some sympathy for Duncan.

Jonathan and I exchange a look.

"Because that's the problem," Mark grumbles from his perch on the dresser.

Jonathan coughs to cover a laugh.

"They hate me! They'll do anything and everything to turn Amara against me." Duncan jolts up. "That's it! They're out to get me!"

"Okay." I clap Duncan on the shoulder. "This has nothing to do with them hating you and everything to do with you not inviting them to their daughter's engagement party."

"They've been nothing but negative the whole time we've been dating. Why would I invite them?"

"Because they're her parents!" I argue.

"Why have the party here in the first place if you didn't want them to know about it?" Mark asks. He's been pretty quiet the whole night with only a comment here or there. "You had to know the Lahiris would hear about it, especially when everyone else in the family was invited. Did you really think this would put you on their good side?"

"Yeah, man. I get that they haven't supported your relationship, but ostracizing them isn't exactly a way to make peace with the future in-laws," Jonathan points out.

"Doesn't really matter if Amara doesn't talk to me again," Duncan grumbles.

"It might help if you tried apologizing." I shrug. "It doesn't change what happened, but at least show some remorse."

"Yeah, I guess."

I really don't think he does. I have a feeling no matter what anyone says that Duncan really doesn't think he did anything wrong. I want to check in on the girls, but what I really mean is, I want to talk to Torrance. We never finished our conversation. I can feel her slipping away.

I pat my knees and stand up. "I need some air."

I grab my jacket and walk out the door without any further explanation.

I'VE WALKED THIS entire property multiple times, and I still feel antsy. I haven't heard from Torrance, even after I texted her. I just keep hoping she'll come outside. I don't want to come across as desperate, but I'm getting to that point. Then I remind myself she's being a friend and roommate, and I feel like the biggest jerk.

There's shuffling behind me, I turn to see Jonathan heading towards me.

"Hey," I try to hide the disappointment in my voice not that I'm fooling anyone.

"Sorry to disappoint," he smirks.

"You did— oh, who am I kidding? I feel like she's bolting." Jonathan nods.

We sit in silence for a few minutes before Jonathan says anything.

"Want my two cents?"

"I'd really like to say I don't, but yes. You know her better than almost anyone. Give it to me straight, am I losing her?"

"Tori doesn't date. It's a choice she made a long time ago. She always said she wouldn't get involved with anyone unless she was certain it could go somewhere. So if she's scared, it's because she cares. Give her space, but let her know you care."

"How do I do that?"

"Do things that let her know you know her. She needs to know she can rely on you. Tori doesn't have a lot of people in her corner. Let her know you're there no matter what. Then let her come to you. If there's one thing Tori is, it's stubborn. She's not going to let you have the last word."

At that I laugh.

"Why are you helping me?"

Jonathan bumps my shoulder. "I like you. Besides, our group could really use some more men—you know, who aren't my brother."

CHAPTER 34

Torrance

I HATE THAT AMARA is going through this, and I hate that Duncan is the reason, but as selfish as it sounds, I'm grateful it gave me an out from that conversation with Porter. It was getting too real. Real makes me nervous...and anxious.

Amara sniffles into the pillow she's been crying into for the last hour and a half. "I'm— sorry—I—mess—ed— up— your— night—" she hiccups.

"You didn't mess up anything," Kiersten soothes as she rubs Amara's back.

"It will all work out," Millie adds.

I haven't said much tonight. I'm not sure I would be any help. Duncan really messed up tonight, and I really wish I could say that I was surprised, but I'm not. This is something he would totally do. And he would do it again. He hasn't even tried to talk to Amara since she ran into the house crying after her parents showed up with some less than favorable words. You know who has messaged? Porter. A couple of times.

"I guess I should probably go talk to my parents," Amara says, sitting up and wiping her eyes.

"Only if you're ready," Kiersten says.

"Do you need us to come with you?" Millie asks.

Amara takes a deep breath. "No. I can go alone. They are my parents. I know they are upset, but I also know they do love me. Even if they don't show it in conventional ways."

"I'll walk with you. I should go find Mark."

Millie and Amara head downstairs, closing the door behind them.

Kiersten turns her all knowing gaze on me.

"Want to tell me why you're running away from Porter?"

"I'm not running away."

"But you're trying to. And don't try denying it. I know you too well, Tor."

I groan. She does know me too well.

"It's all just moving so fast."

"One could argue the contrary."

I quirk my eyebrow. "How so?"

"In your words, Porter annoying you the last nine years could be construed as the two of you fighting feelings for a better part of a decade."

"I haven't been fighting feelings. I genuinely couldn't stand him."

"No, you didn't understand him, and things that you don't understand get under your skin. You don't like not being in control."

"You make it sound like I've been subconsciously pining for him and haven't dated or even liked anyone in all those years."

"Real talk?"

I nod.

"Yes. I think you have subconsciously made yourself unavailable to men or only developed feelings for people who were never going to commit." She takes my hand. "Like my brother."

My head snaps up. "Not this again."

"And you're still avoiding talking about the hard stuff." She gives my hand a squeeze. "Ollie cared about you, but the hard reality is, he didn't deserve you, Tor. He was my brother, and I love and miss him every day, but that doesn't mean I thought he was perfect. He was far from it." Kiersten's voice cracks with emotion. "You can't keep putting your life on hold wondering what could have been. Porter pushes you. He doesn't back down when you go after him. Even when you're arguing, he brings out a fire in you that you don't always show. Isn't that what you've always said you wanted?"

I wipe at my cheeks, trying to catch the tears.

Kiersten wraps me up in a hug. "Hey, no tears."

I lean my head on her shoulder. "I think I might have really messed things up."

"He's stuck around this long. Do you really think he'd give up that easily?"

She's right. Porter has been nothing but patient this week as I've processed. Who am I kidding? Kiersten's right about a lot more than that. Porter has never once backed down over the years when I was snarky. Even now that I know him better, or I guess especially now, I see just how much he hasn't backed down but rather rose to meet me snark for snark. He's been nothing but straightforward with me the last few days about what he wants.

I guess now it's my turn to figure out what I really want. And hope it isn't too late once I do.

CHAPTER 35

Text Messages

PORTER: Goodnight, Tor. No need to message me back. I know today's been a lot. I just wanted you to know I was thinking of you.

TORRANCE: Goodnight, Po.

Two hours later

TORRANCE: Sorry. I know it's late. I just want you to know...actually, I don't know what I want you to know. I guess I just want to say, don't give up on me.

PORTER: I'm awake.

PORTER: I'll wait as long as you need.

CHAPTER 36

Porter

PORTER: I know it's early. Just wanted you to know I'm heading out this morning, going to stop by my grandparents' place for a couple days. Have a safe flight back tomorrow. See you when we both get back?

TORRANCE: Safe travels. Have a good visit with your family.

TORRANCE: I'll see you when we're both back.

PORTER: Permission to text while you think things through?

PORTER: I don't want to push you into anything you're not ready for.

When I pull into my grandparents' driveway, I sit in the car for a bit. It's a much different feeling from the last time I was here. Even if it was only two days ago.

There's a rap on my window, taking me out of my thoughts. My grandfather motions for me to follow him then walks away before I even release my seatbelt.

Grandpa Gentry doesn't stop until he reaches the horse pasture. He's there waiting for me when I walk up.

"Are you chasin' for answers or runnin' from questions?"

"Neither. I'm giving space."

"Son, you've had years of space. If you're going to just give up at the first sign of trouble, then you aren't the man I raised you to be."

"I'm not giving up, Grandpa, I'm just giving her time to decide what she wants."

"And what is it that *you* want?"

"Her."

I SPEND THE next couple of days in Grantsville with my family trying, and failing, to get my mind off of Torrance. No matter how much farm work my grandpa pushes off on me to do, I can't get her off of my mind. Each and every passing moment, I'm more and more certain of what I want. I just don't know what else I can do to prove to her I'm serious about not going anywhere.

I've been trying to follow Jonathan's advice and let her know I care, but I don't know what else I can do other than texting her. At least while I'm still in Tennessee. Once I get home, well, then I don't know. I don't exactly have a plan of action.

But I'm not giving up without a fight.

CHAPTER 37

Torrance

> **JONATHAN:** You available for lunch today?

> **TORI:** I am, but don't you have school?

> **JONATHAN:** Teacher in-service run by the department heads, and since my department head is 9 months from retirement…

> **TORI:** You don't have in-service?

> **JONATHAN:** Bingo

> **JONATHAN:** Meet at the new Korean BBQ place?

I end up pulling into the parking lot at the same time as Jonathan, which is fortuitous since parking is scarce. We end up snagging two of the last spots available.

"Hey, Tor." Jonathan gives me a hug. "Thanks for coming to lunch with me."

"Thanks for the invite. I needed out of Wade."

"Crazy day?"

"You could say that. Something is going on upstairs, but I have no idea what it is. Not that I get to know any of those details. My babysitting duties keep me pretty occupied. But there's just this ominous feeling throughout the whole office."

"Wade's sons are still keeping you busy then?"

"Ugh! I'm not sure how much more I can handle. I've had multiple complaints related to them just this morning. I'd quit, but I don't know of anyone hiring. Especially not at the rate that Wade does."

We go back and forth about our different work woes as we wait to be seated. Turns out teaching high school and babysitting billionaires isn't that different.

When our food is brought out, we eat in relative silence which isn't normal for us, but it doesn't feel awkward. At least it's not until Jonathan decides to change the subject.

"Tor, what are you doing?"

I look at him confused. "Eating my bulgogi?"

"Not that, you noob. What are you doing about Porter?"

I stiffen at the mention of his name. It's not like I've been avoiding thinking about him; in fact, it's all I can do. He's messaged me every day for the last week. I haven't messaged him back. I don't know what to say.

"I'm figuring it out," I finally say.

"You're shutting him out."

"No, I'm not."

"Torrance."

I don't like the tone he uses as he says my full name. "Don't use your teacher voice on me! I'm not one of your students!"

"Then stop acting like them! You're freezing him out so it's Porter who leaves."

"I am thinking things through!"

"No, you aren't. If you were, you'd see he's been nothing but supportive from the very beginning. Instead, you're determined to prove you were right all along. That people don't stay around. People leave even if you don't pushed them away... Only you are pushing him away."

I glare at him. "I am not."

He gives a long sigh. "Yes, you are. And if you aren't careful you're going to be successful. The man can only be so patient. At least text him back once in a while. Let him know where your head is."

"I don't know where my head is— how did you know he's been texting me? I haven't told anyone."

Jonathan gets a sheepish look on his face for the briefest of moments before it turns into a smirk.

"We've been hanging out since he got back from Tennessee."

"You and Porter?"

"Yeah. I like him. We're friends. And he could really use one about now."

Guilt racks through me. I have my own issues to work through, but I hate that I've put Porter through any of this.

And hate that I've put Jonathan in the middle of it. Add it to the list of things I've messed up lately.

The edge of my vision starts to get hazy, and breathing is getting more difficult. In the midst of my spiraling, I've caused myself to go into a panic attack. I reach up to my necklace and start rubbing the smooth pendent between my fingers. I'm trying to focus on the coolness of the metal between my fingers when Jonathan's arms wrap around me, and he rubs my back.

"Hey. It's okay. Just breathe. That's it. In. And out. In. Out. Good."

When I'm finally able to control my breathing, Jonathan releases me.

"Anxiety attacks are starting again?"

I nod.

"How long have they been back?" His voice is laced with concern.

"They never fully went away, but they've been more frequent the last several months."

"Tor."

"I know."

"It's not weakness to ask for help. You would do anything for those you care about. Let us do the same for you."

I nod as I wipe the tear rolling down my cheek.

"That includes Porter."

I look at Jonathan and see the concern written all over his face.

"I don't know how."

"Yes, you do. You're just too stubborn to admit it."

PORTER: I saw a Jeep loaded with rubber ducks today. Not going to lie, I really thought you were making that up.

TORRANCE: Nope. It's a real thing.

PORTER: Hey. You actually answered. Maybe I should have called you a liar sooner.

TORRANCE: Sorry. I should have responded earlier. I just…don't know what to say.

PORTER: Doesn't have to be anything deep. Our conversation can be as surface-level as you want it to be. I don't want to push you.

PORTER: I'm also not willing to give up without a fight.

TORRANCE: You do like to fight.

PORTER: Only with you.

Four hours later:

PORTER: Did you see that Pretty in Pink is playing on TV tonight?

TORRANCE: Of course I did. Are you watching? Or do you have work?

PORTER: I have work, but a couple of our patients have it on in their rooms, so I've gotten glimpses.

TORRANCE: Well, that's better than nothing. You still need to watch the whole thing at some point.

PORTER: How about we make it a date? Or is that pushing you too hard? I'm well out of my depth here, Torrance. I don't know what is too much and what isn't enough. I'm flying blind here. If it gets to be too much, I need you to be honest with me.

TORRANCE: You're not being too much.

CHAPTER 38

Text Messages

PORTER: This week has been never ending. Overtime might be the death of me.

TORRANCE: I'll trade you. If I have to have one more meeting with an intern who doesn't understand that it is in fact their job to do what their boss asks them to do, I might pull my hair out.

PORTER: Don't do that. I like your hair.

TORRANCE: I'll keep my hair if you don't die.

PORTER: Deal.

CHAPTER 39

Torrance

I'M NOT SURE why I thought coming to Valley Creek was the best place to get some perspective while also getting some space from my friends. The whole house has been in a funk since the engagement party. Everyone is walking on eggshells around Amara, not sure what to say. She and Duncan aren't talking. Then add in that no one dares ask what's going on between me and Porter because the couple of times they have, I all but bit their heads off. To say we are all on edge is a gross understatement. In all the time that we have known and lived with each other, we have never had this level of disagreement. So instead of the usual happy and light feelings that are typical of our house, it's all rain clouds and silence. I couldn't take it anymore, even if *some* of it is my fault, so I told everyone I was going to visit my sister, and I left.

As soon as I pulled in the driveway, I knew I was in for it. Carson was waiting for me on the porch. I was expecting Aly to come running out to greet me, but she never came.

"They aren't home. Bonnie and Aly are out with Jasper," Carson says, sensing exactly what I was wondering. "We need to talk."

"Why do I feel like I'm not going to like this?"

"I have a feeling you're going to hate it, but as your sister, I feel it is my duty to make sure you don't ruin your life."

I roll my eyes. "No need to be so dramatic."

She stands up and crosses her arms with the sternest look I have ever seen her give. "And there's no need for you to be so blasé about running away from the best thing that has ever happened to you."

I let out a groan of frustration, "Why does everyone keep saying that?!"

"Because you're being ridiculous! And it isn't fair to Porter." Carson steps down to meet me on the bottom step and grabs my hand. "You wouldn't be so frustrated with everything if you didn't, on some level, know that everyone was right. You're scared of making a mistake, and instead of facing your fears, you're running away."

"I know no one believes me, but I'm not doing it on purpose."

"I know." Carson pulls me into an all-encompassing hug. "Want to come inside and talk through the thought process? We have the whole afternoon. Plus I was craving tacos, and I made way too many. I'll never be able to get rid of all the evidence on my own before Bonnie gets back."

I give a small nod and head into the house. I might not want to talk, but I can always eat.

Two hours and more tacos than I will ever admit to eating in one sitting later, I have cried more tears than I have in the previous twenty-seven years of my life. My whole heart and soul are raw. It took some not-so-gentle prodding, but once the walls were down, the floodgates opened and everything came out. Everything from my fears of being left behind to my trepidation over failure. I even opened up about everything that happened with Oliver. Other than Porter, I've never talked about it with anyone.

I cried the most tears over Porter. The realization that I am, in fact, in love with the man was almost more than I could handle. That despite everything he, for whatever reason, wants to be with me too. It's a lot.

Carson and I had everything cleaned up before Bonnie and Aly got home, and we had a relaxing night as a family. Once everyone headed to bed, Carson came into my room to check on me. We spent a majority of the night coming up with ideas of what I can do to prove to Porter that I'm done running. In all the romance books and movies, it might typically be the man who has to make grand gestures, but in this case, just call me *NSYNC, because it's gonna be me.

CHAPTER 40

Porter

THIS WEEK HAS been brutal. My nerves are shot. Sure, work has been crazy, but I'm mostly emotionally spent. I thought that things might be looking up once Torrance finally texted me back, but we're still just stuck in the land of the unknown.

Yesterday I finally had enough and decided to heck with it. I went over to her place to make her talk to me, but when I knocked on the door, I was met with the most awkward encounter with Amara I have ever had, on top of finding out that Torrance wasn't home. She went to Valley Creek, and no one knew when she would be back.

I guess that's what I get for trying to respect her space and pace, but now I'm worried that what I really did was make her think that I'm apathetic about the whole situation.

I'm in a full mental overhaul of the entirety of our acquaintance when my phone buzzes next to me. I freeze when I see Torrance's name on the screen. My hands are jittery, and my heart is slamming against my chest as I pick up the phone to open the message.

> **TORRANCE:** Do you work tonight?

> **PORTER:** No. Finally have a day off.

> **TORRANCE:** Any plans?

I'm cautiously optimistic at her question, but I also don't want to scare her off. I know I was talking a big game earlier about making her talk to me, but I'm so far gone for this woman, I'm pretty much desperate for anything she'll give me at this point. Besides, it's got to be a good sign that she not only messaged me first this time, but also with an opene-ended question and follow up. Right?

> **PORTER:** Just taking my dogs for a walk.

There. That's casual. And it's true.

> **TORRANCE:** Want some company?

YES!

> **PORTER:** I was going to go in about fifteen minutes. Want me to wait?

As soon as I hit send on my last text to Torrance, there's a knock on my door. I swear if that's Trent, I might just kill him. Okay, so I wouldn't, but only because he could take me down in a nanosecond. I don't want anything to get in the way of Torrance actually wanting to see me in person.

We have briefly talked over text, but it's been three weeks since I've seen her. Since I've heard her voice.

I open the door, and it takes everything in me to not let my jaw drop in shock.

"Hi."

"Torrance." I stare at her awkwardly before I remember my manners and let her inside. "You got here fast."

Seriously? We haven't seen each other in weeks, and *that's* my opening line?

She bites her bottom lip, bringing my attention to her mouth. It's so distracting that I miss her response. "I'm sorry. What did you say?"

She laughs softly. "I said I was in your hallway when your text came in."

I smile. "You were?"

She nods. "I've missed you."

"I've missed you too. I didn't want to push."

Torrance shakes her head. "You didn't."

Suki and Banjo come bounding in the room. Honestly, I'm surprised it took them this long. Usually they're ready to pounce on whoever comes through the door.

"Oh! Aren't you just the sweetest?" Torrance coos as she scratches the top of Banjo's head. Not wanting to be ignored, Suki nuzzles her way between them, giving Torrance's hand a lick. "Thank you for the kisses." She looks up at me with a big smile. "They're so cute!"

I chuckle. "They like you."

Torrance stands up straight and looks at me. "And what about their owner? Do you like me, or did I mess everything up?" She sniffles as she tries to hold back tears. I step closer and take her hands in mine. "I'm mean. I'm loud. I'm stubborn. I judge too quickly, and I always have to have the last word. I—"

I pull her closer to me, cutting her off. "Not to cut your monologue short, but I think you asked me a question, and I'd really like to answer."

"Do you still like me?"

I trace a finger up her arm, cupping her face. "No, I don't like you, Torrance." A tear starts to fall, and I wipe it with my thumb. "I love you. I've always loved you. I was just too blind to see what was right in front of me."

Torrance moves my hand from her face and brings it to her lips as she kisses my palm, sending an electric shock straight to my heart. "I didn't exactly make it easy."

"True." I kiss one damp cheek, then the other. "You know what, I wouldn't have had it any other way."

"Really?"

"Really."

"I'm sorry I pushed you away. I—"

"I'm scared too."

"You are?"

"Out of my mind." I wrap her in my arms and pull her close. "But I'm more scared of losing you forever."

"Me too," she whispers, and it's enough of an invitation that I close the gap between us pressing my lips against hers. She doesn't hesitate to reciprocate, and it's the first time since our night under the stars that things seem to settle within me. This is where I belong. With Torrance.

Before I can deepen the kiss further, Torrance pulls back slightly.

"What is it?" My voice is raspy with want.

She wraps her arms around my neck and looks up into my eyes. "I was just thinking what exemplary vegetables potatoes are."

I groan, and Torrance laughs.

"Porter," Torrance's face turns serious as she runs her hand along my jaw, "I love you."

And then she's kissing me with abandon. Each kiss a new promise. And I respond with my own.

Torrance

7 Months Later

"TOR, WILL YOU hurry up!" Porter calls from the front seat of my Jeep.

"I'm coming, I'm coming." I was ready fifteen minutes ago, but it's just too much fun making my boyfriend wait. What can I say, annoying him is my love language.

"If we're going to make it to Valley Creek before dark, then we need to get on the road."

"I was finishing my playlist." I hop into the passenger seat like the passenger princess that I am.

"Of course you were," Porter grumbles under his breath, making me smile.

"I also packed snacks!" I beam at him as he levels me with a stare that doesn't scare me in the slightest. "Don't worry, I packed more than what you like to call junk. I also have jerky, grapes, carrots, and I even packed some protein bars."

"*You* packed protein bars?" He looks at me in disbelief.

"Sure did. See?" I pull out the package.

"Torrance, that's a Snickers bar."

"Which has peanuts. Which is protein. I'm so much more health conscious since we started dating." I can't contain my laugh any longer with him staring at me like that.

"Are you done?"

I lean over and give him a short peck on the cheek. "For now."

Porter puts the car into drive as I get my phone hooked up to the sound system. I watch for his reaction as the first notes of the Teletubbies theme song starts to play. I can see his lips twitching as he fights a smile.

"Po!" I scream as I sing along.

"You're ridiculous," he says as he takes my hand, pressing it to his lips.

"Ridiculously in love with you." I turn up my nose at the cheese factor of my own statement. It's true, but there has to be a better way of saying it. Oh, well. Guess I have the rest of my life to figure that out.

The End.

TRAVELING WITH TORRANCE SURVIVAL GUIDE

By: Millie Jacobson Winters

1. No early mornings
2. Approach with caution before caffeine
3. Keep fed, hanger is a real thing
4. Music is your best friend
5. No audiobooks—she likes them, but will complain she doesn't. NOT WORTH IT.
6. Snacks must be available at all times (see 2)
7. Naps are necessary—her, not you, unless you like to nap then go for it (as long as you're not driving)

See individual binder sections for more detail

Happy Travels and Good Luck!

CHARACTER GLOSSARY

TORRANCE (TORI) RODRIGUEZ – Protective older sister, loyal friend, works in Human Resources

PORTER COLLINS – Loyal to a fault, dog dad to two, Oncology Nurse, working towards becoming a Physician Assistant

MILLIE (JACOBSON) WINTERS – Torrance's best friend since childhood, and former roommate

JONATHAN WINTERS – Torrance's best friend since childhood, becomes friends with Porter

KIERSTEN DAVIES – Torrance's roommate and friend since college

AMARA LAHIRI – Torrance's roommate and friend since college, engaged to Duncan

TRINA COLE – Torrance's newest roommate, moves in after Millie gets married

DUNCAN SULLIVAN – Porter's best friend and collage roommate, engaged to Amara

OMA AND PAPA O. – Amara's grandparents who live in Tennessee

CARSON RODRIGUEZ – Torrance's younger sister, lives with Bonnie, mother of Aly

ALEXANDRIA (ALY) RODRIGUEZ – Torrance's four-year-old niece, Carson's daughter, loves to use nicknames

BONNIE LEMAIRE – Torrance and Carson's grandmother, French, dislikes anything Spanish

ZION COLLINS – Porter's little sister, college student, sings in a band

MARMAR – Porter's grandmother

GRANDPA GENTRY – Porter's grandfather

ANNIE COLLINS – Porter and Zion's mother, cancer survivor, lives with MarMar and Grandpa Gentry (her parents)

TRENT TALBOT – Porter's cousin, NFL player

SLOANE HENRY – Trent's girlfriend

RYAN MCCONNELL – Trent's teammate, friends with Porter

MARK WINTERS – Millie's husband, Jonathan's brother

SUKI AND BANJO – Porter's dogs

ACKNOWLEDGMENTS

Thank you to everyone who has given Torrance and Porter a chance. To my readers who have loved and supported my characters and are excited to meet them as they each get their own story. Who have shared posts and recommended my books to friends. It's crazy to think that there are some out there who have even re-read things that I have written multiple times.

 Thank you for shipping relationships (even if those relationships will never be—sorry, Team Jonathan and Tori)

Thank you to my Sara Beth Schneider for all of the encouragement and patience as we work together on edits. Thank you to Stephanie Anderson and Alt 19 Creative for the amazing work on the cover and formatting.

Thank you, Mom, and the rest of my family and friends for always supporting me and my dreams. Even when I hyper-fixate and can't seem to talk about anything else at the moment. Even more when I can't focus on a singular topic and jump ship mid-sentence.

And a special shout-out to Becca Watkins for always being my first reader and bouncing board when it comes to ideas. And for sending memes and reels that are "this is so ___".

Lastly, thank you to the new readers. Thank you for giving me and my characters a chance.

Happy Reading!

Love, Amy

MEET THE AUTHOR

California born and raised, current Texas resident. Amy studied Early Childhood and Special Education at Snow College and Brigham Young University Idaho. Amy is an early childhood teacher, an avid reader, and is a trained choral singer. When she isn't writing, Amy enjoys cooking, baking, and spending time with her golden doodle, Bennet.